CW00860410

ANIMAL FARM
USA

A CAUTIONARY TALE

STEPHEN KLOEPFER

ARCHWAY
PUBLISHING

Copyright © 2020 Stephen Kloepfer.

All rights reserved. No part of this book may be used
or reproduced by any means, graphic, electronic, or
mechanical, including photocopying, recording, taping or
by any information storage retrieval system without the
written permission of the author except in the case of brief
quotations embodied in critical articles and reviews.

This is a work of fiction. All of the characters, names, incidents,
organizations, and dialogue in this novel are either the
products of the author's imagination or are used fictitiously.

Archway Publishing books may be ordered
through booksellers or by contacting:

Archway Publishing
1663 Liberty Drive
Bloomington, IN 47403
www.archwaypublishing.com
1 (888) 242-5904

Because of the dynamic nature of the Internet, any web
addresses or links contained in this book may have changed
since publication and may no longer be valid. The views
expressed in this work are solely those of the author and do
not necessarily reflect the views of the publisher, and the
publisher hereby disclaims any responsibility for them.

Any people depicted in stock imagery provided by
Getty Images are models, and such images are
being used for illustrative purposes only.
Certain stock imagery © Getty Images.

Cover Photo: Dusan Petkovic / Shutterstock.com

ISBN: 978-1-4808-9007-7 (sc)
ISBN: 978-1-4808-9006-0 (hc)
ISBN: 978-1-4808-9008-4 (e)

Library of Congress Control Number: 2020907569

Print information available on the last page.

Archway Publishing rev. date: 5/7/2020

For Carol, April, and Tilly

The noble experiment in animal self-rule had ended badly. After the animals rebelled and overthrew Jones, the hated owner of a small farm in the southeast of England, the pigs–led by a fierce Berkshire boar named Napoleon–seized all power and privilege at the farm and ended up tyrannizing the other animals more harshly than Jones ever had. In the ensuing years of despotic pig rule, the horses, cows, goats, chickens, cats, donkeys, geese, birds, and sheep were hard-pressed to distinguish pig from man, or man from pig. The animals' Rebellion had become, for everyone except the pigs and their vicious guard dogs, a cruel irony.

But the pigs' duplicity and treachery at Animal Farm sowed the seeds for the establishment of more benevolent animal-led communities in England, the United States, Canada, and other countries.

Snowball–the prize Gloucester boar who had helped to plan and execute the Rebellion before being expelled by Napoleon–narrowly escaped to a neighboring farm and began plotting a counter-rebellion that would rekindle the dream of a farm run solely for the benefit of the animals and where no pig, or human, would rule over them.

One moonless night, as Napoleon and his fellow pigs slept off another wild night of carousing, poker playing, and heavy drinking, Snowball slipped through a hole in a boundary hedge and quietly roused his comrades of old.

Clover, Benjamin, and Moses, the only animals (except the pigs) who remembered the joyous early days of the Rebellion, struggled at first to recognize Snowball, whom they had not seen in many years. But as their dim memories began to jog, they remembered Snowball's bravery during the decisive Battle of the Cowshed and greeted him warmly.

Snowball explained to them that just as their beloved comrade, Old Major, only days before his death, had had a strange dream of the earth as it would be when Man had been vanquished, Snowball had also had a dream.

"But my dream, comrades, was not like Major's dream. Since being expelled by Napoleon, I have had a lot of time to think. Napoleon's betrayals and his attempts to have me killed caused me to think deeply about how we can protect ourselves, not only against treacherous humans but also against treacherous pigs who share the humans' desire to dominate and enslave. Major was a wise and honorable pig and his dream was noble. But it was mistaken. Man will not vanish from the earth. And if Man does vanish, the rest of us will almost certainly vanish too. Man will be around for as long as we are around. We need to find a way to make our peace with him. What Man understands, and what pigs like Napoleon understand, is power. We animals *have* power, if only we can summon the courage and intelligence to use it."

Snowball's ragtag audience of an old brood mare, an irascible donkey, a tame raven, and a few itinerant blackbirds who had flitted into the barn and alighted on a beam next to the lantern that hung from it, did not understand what Snowball was saying and were too ill-fed and exhausted to venture any questions. But for the first time in a long time, someone had shown up who seemed genuine in wanting to help them. That much they did understand.

"Please go on, Snowball," Clover said softly. "Tell us about your dream."

"I dreamed that while as I was foraging for food on Pilkington's farm, trying to avoid being seen by Pilkington and his men, I looked up and saw thousands of ravens, crows, blackbirds, magpies, and pigeons perching themselves, wing to wing, on the tree branches, roofs, hedgerows, and power lines of Animal Farm and neighboring farms, as far as the eye could see, while a vast, undulating black cloud of birds appeared on the horizon and blotted out the sun. I dreamed that while the skies were darkening, all of the animals from the surrounding farms were massing along the boundary fences. I dreamed that the pigs and their human workers–who had reached for their shotguns and were wielding them menacingly–surveyed the frightening scene and then dropped their weapons. In the final part of my dream, the pigs hurriedly gathered up whatever personal items they could carry and drove off with the humans without a single shot being fired. As an old truck crowded with pigs and humans drove away from the farmhouse and toward the main road, the young farmhand who was driving stopped the truck, got out, and quickly closed the five-barred gate behind him. Then I woke up."

Clover, Benjamin, and Moses had listened with rapt attention but were confused.

"What does it all mean, Snowball?" asked Benjamin.

"I am not sure, Benjamin. But what it might mean is this: if we collaborate with one another in ways that animals have never done before, we can use our strength and our strength in numbers to better our lives and keep ourselves safe. There are many more of *us* than there are pigs or humans. The humans have an idea they call 'collective security,' where countries join together to prevent aggression against any member of the group. We need to take a page out of the humans' book and use collective security to protect ourselves against the pigs *and* the humans."

Moses, an aged raven who was quicker on the uptake than Clover and Benjamin and who was no stranger to utopian dreams that seemed never to come true, was skeptical. "But Snowball, the pigs have guns and ferocious guard dogs and human workers paid to do their bidding. Collective security sounds good, but how can we make it work for *us*? We are only an old horse, an old donkey, and an old raven, and the pigs and humans give us and the other farm animals only enough food to keep us alive for another day's hard labor. I fear that your dream is just more pie-in-the-sky that, like Major's, will end up breaking our hearts, and our spirits."

"That is a fair point, Moses," Snowball replied, "and I'm glad you raised it–because you will play a critical role in what is to come. But before I get to that, let me ask you all a question. Do you remember that night many years ago when Clover and some of the other animals went up to the farmhouse to see what Napoleon was doing with the local farmers who had arrived in cars earlier in the day to tour the windmill and the rest of the farm?"

Clover remembered, but was puzzled. "I remember that night, Snowball. But you were not there. That was long after Napoleon had tried to kill you and long after you had fled and were never heard from again. After you were gone, Napoleon told us that even in the early days of the Rebellion, when you still lived with us, you were Pilkington's spy and were secretly working against us–and that, later, Pilkington caught you trying to set fire to his henhouse and shot you dead."

"Napoleon lied about that and about many other things," Snowball replied, shaking his head. "But given the way things turned out, that should not surprise you. I have been in hiding these many years, mostly on Pilkington's farm, in the dense thicket next to the fence beside the turnip field. And I *was* there that night, Clover, but I took care not to be seen. Earlier that day, I had seen Napoleon and the farmers touring the windmill and the barley fields and then go back to the farmhouse. That struck me as very odd. Since the day we kicked Jones out, I had never seen *any* humans at Animal Farm, let alone humans being treated as guests. Later that evening, I heard shouts of laughter and bursts of singing coming from the farmhouse. So I slipped through a hole in the hedge to check it out. That's when I saw you and some of the other animals peering in at the dining-room window."

"Snowball," Benjamin cut in, "we are very thankful you are still alive. But what does that long-ago night of carousing by the pigs and the humans have to do with your dream or with how we can take the farm back?"

Snowball was ready for that question. "Benjamin, do you remember the pigs and the humans all sitting around the long table in the dining room, with Napoleon at its head? Do you remember all of them holding small, rectangular pieces of colored paper in their hands?"

"Yes," Benjamin said, "and I remember asking Clover what the colored pieces of paper were for. Our best guess was that the pigs were playing some kind of game with the humans but that's as far as our thinking went. I remember Pilkington standing up and making a little speech directed at Napoleon and the pigs and raising his beer glass, and the pigs and the humans toasting and clapping their hands together–and then Napoleon standing up and making a little speech directed at Pilkington and the humans and raising *his* beer glass, followed by some more toasting and hand-clapping. After the pigs and humans drank some more beer and played some more with the colored pieces of paper, an uproar of voices broke out, followed by shouted epithets and overturned furniture. Napoleon picked up a beer glass and threw it at Pilkington's head, but Pilkington ducked just in time and the beer glass cracked the dining-room window. With the violent quarrel threatening to spill out onto the farmhouse garden, we all fled to our sleeping places and never spoke of the incident again. That's all I remember."

"The pigs and humans were playing a card game called poker," Snowball explained. "The rules of that game do not matter. What matters is the idea of 'bluffing,' which is a big part of a winning poker strategy. Bluffing is when you don't hold very valuable cards in your hand but convince the other players that the cards you hold are very valuable indeed and cause them to 'fold' their hands and give you the win–even though they may have had better cards than you did. The key to taking back the farm is simply this: given the animals' great superiority in numbers relative to the pigs and the humans, we hold a very strong hand. But the humans, and later the pigs, have bluffed us into thinking that they hold a stronger hand than we do. So what have we done? We have folded and let them treat us as they will. If we want better lives for ourselves and our little ones, we can't do that anymore. We need to show the pigs and the humans how strong a hand we really have and play that hand out. That's where my dream comes in."

It was rare for Benjamin to agree with anyone, but Benjamin was beginning to catch on and gave Snowball a short but unmistakable nod. Moses and Clover were now more intrigued than skeptical and wanted to hear more. Clover thought about how her beloved friend, Boxer, the dim-witted but admirable cart-horse who had been Animal Farm's most loyal and indefatigable worker, had been murdered by the pigs as soon as he was no longer of use to them—and about how wonderful it would be if the farm animals could rise up and rid themselves of the pigs, just as they had rid themselves of Jones.

"You have our full attention, Snowball," Moses said. "Tell us about your plan and how it's connected to your dream. You mentioned that I would play a critical role in that plan, so I'll want to hear about that too. And Snowball, as it must be obvious to you, Clover, Benjamin, and I are old, underfed, and in poor shape. The three of us are already living on borrowed time. If we are to play our part in this, we need to do it soon."

As Moses was speaking, Snowball noticed a short, black, leather-covered stick lying in the dirt a few feet inside the barn door. Snowball pointed to it with his trotter. "What is that?"

"That's one of Napoleon's whips," Clover replied. "Napoleon has taken to carrying a whip in his trotter when he tours the farm, accompanied by guard dogs with brass-studded collars. He's never used the whip on me and I've never seen him use it on any other animal. But I think he carries it around with him, and cracks it against his backside, to remind us 'who's boss'–and to let us know that he won't hesitate using it, or worse, if we don't do his bidding."

"And after Napoleon's little tours, in which he makes sneering faces but speaks no words, he sometimes leaves the whip behind in the fields or in one of the barns, so we'll keep him in our thoughts between visits," Benjamin added. "Napoleon must have a lot of whips."

Snowball's face betrayed an expression of bitter anger. He picked up the whip, broke it violently in two, and kicked the pieces against the barn wall. "Comrades, remember this moment. Years from now, our descendants will talk about how the counter-rebellion started with the breaking of that whip. And Moses, I, too, am old and infirm. Living hoof to mouth these past years, in exile, never sure whether I could forage enough food to survive the day passing over me, has also shortened *my* life. So I agree that we need to act quickly.

Recall my dream. We need all of the birds and animals on Animal Farm and on the neighboring farms to show up in force at an appointed time in the next few days and signal to Napoleon what he and the other pigs are in for if they don't lay down their arms and hand the farm back to us. Surprise, speed, and an overwhelming show of force are essential. And let me be blunt. There is no guarantee that this will work. If it doesn't work, many birds and animals, doubtless ourselves included, will be killed during the battle or executed after the battle and conditions on the farms will be worse than they are now. And even if my plan does work, there are certain to be casualties, just as there were when we fought to kick Jones out and then fought again to keep him out. But unless our only legacy to our children and grandchildren is lives that are brutal, miserable, and short, I do not see any other way. It's now or never. Are we agreed?"

Clover, Benjamin, and Moses exchanged long, meaningful looks and then nodded their agreement.

"We are agreed, Snowball," Clover said. "What do we need to do?"

"I have been watching the pigs and humans closely. During weekdays, especially, their movements are very regular. The pigs and humans take their lunch at twelve noon in the farmhouse dining room and don't show up again in the barns and fields until three o'clock. So the best time to launch the plan is two o'clock in the afternoon, when the pigs and humans are eating their midday meal and have a few beers in them. Today is Monday and we'll need a few days to get organized. 'Zero hour' will be this Friday at two o'clock. I have some trusted friends and contacts on the neighboring farms and will take care of getting those animals briefed and ready to go. Clover and Benjamin, you need to do the same for your comrades here. At two o'clock on Friday, they all need to start running to the boundary fence next to the turnip field. Don't tell them the reason for that, just make up some kind of plausible story. And remember, secrecy is key. Whatever you tell them, make sure they understand that they are to tell no pig or human, under any circumstances. Is that clear?"

"Yes, very clear," said Clover, as Benjamin nodded his assent.

"What about *me*?" Moses asked testily.

"Moses," answered Snowball, "your role is mission-critical. Recall how the birds dominated my dream. We need you to get the word out to all of your raven friends and also to the crows, blackbirds, magpies, and pigeons and all of *their* winged friends. At two o'clock on Friday, we need them to line up on the tree branches and along all of the power lines and on the fields and the roofs and the hedgerows, and for still more groups of birds to band together in large flocks and fly toward the farm from as many directions as possible. The birds you enlist must be very careful not to let the pigs and humans know what we're up to. When the four of us meet again on Thursday night, you can tell us whether you've persuaded enough birds to show up on Friday–because, if you haven't, the plan is doomed and we'll have to cancel it and regroup. The one thing that will make the pigs and humans throw down their arms and quit the field is a sky blanketed by thousands of birds, whose mere presence will terrify them. Without that fear factor, it's likely they'll decide to engage us and pick us off, one by one, with their shotguns. From my time on Pilkington's farm, I have developed some raven and magpie friendships. So if you need any help rounding up support, please let me know."

Moses, in his long and peripatetic life as a raven, had got to know hundreds of ravens and other birds who lived in or around Animal Farm or on one of the surrounding farms or who overflew those farms from time to time en route to destinations in England or elsewhere in Great Britain, or to or from locations across the Irish Sea and the English Channel. Moses was confident that the birds would answer the call and that there would be more than enough "air cover" to permit the plan to go forward. "Snowball, I expect to be able to give you a very favorable report on Thursday night."

"Good," Snowball replied. "We all have our assigned tasks. Let's meet again here on Thursday night and see where we are. Thank you, comrades. Good night."

To the pigs at Animal Farm, and to the humans who worked on the adjoining farms, the next three days were uneventful and seemed even quieter and more orderly than usual. The farm beasts discharged their daily tasks with their usual uncomplaining efficiency and Napoleon's Thursday afternoon tour of Animal Farm, with his snarling guard dogs in tow, was greeted by the other animals with their customary shows of submission and obeisance. Napoleon was especially gratified when one of the young sheep picked up, in his teeth, the whip Napoleon had just thrown down on the sheep pasture and then held it up with pride so the other sheep could see it. Napoleon had long become accustomed to ostentatious shows of flattery and abject obedience and was pleased with the sheep's performance, considering it nothing more than his just due.

The more observant pigs did notice, on each of the three afternoons following Snowball's nocturnal visit, an unusual number and variety of birds flying overhead and intermittently alighting and then taking off again from power lines and tree branches, but gave the matter no serious thought. And when their pig bosses were not looking, two of the younger farmhands paused to admire the grace and precision with which small flocks of birds–some of which were non-native and had never before been seen at Animal Farm–coordinated their crisp takeoffs and landings.

When Snowball met again with Clover, Benjamin, and Moses, as planned, on the third night following their initial meeting, none of them reported any concern that Napoleon or any other pig or human had learned of their plan. The two-legged and four-legged animals at Animal Farm and on the adjoining farms had been fully briefed and were ready to go. Even the ants, beetles, spiders, and other insects had agreed to play their part. Moses was excited to report that he had received more pledges from the ravens, crows, blackbirds, magpies, pigeons, and other birds than he had expected and that birds from Ireland, France, and Germany might also lend their assistance. Indeed, Moses had it on good authority that some of them had already started on their long journeys toward Animal Farm from their native countries, so that they might reach the farm by the appointed time the next day.

Snowball nodded gravely. "All is in readiness. It's a 'go' for two o'clock tomorrow afternoon. Please inform the comrades. We should adjourn now and get some sleep–because tomorrow will be a defining day in the history, and future, of Animal Farm."

CHAPTER 2

Moses had done his job well–perhaps *too* well.

As they peered incredulously through their binoculars and thumbed the dog-eared pages of their bird guides, a few scattered groups of bird watchers strolling the White Cliffs of Dover and along the coastal footpaths of Pendeen in west Cornwall knew that something extraordinary was afoot, or rather, in flight.

At a Government Communications Headquarters installation on the north Cornwall coast, the highly-trained technicians who operated the giant satellite dishes that lined the cliff tops at Bude had arrived at the same conclusion.

Large flocks of birds from across the English Channel and the Irish Sea were flying inland in regular waves and at low altitudes every nine or ten minutes and the migratory patterns were all wrong.

Throughout the morning and early afternoon of Snowball's appointed launch day, reports of large-scale, orderly bird migrations, from seemingly all points of the compass and always in the direction of southeast England, flooded into local police stations, into the Ministry of Defense, and into various offices of the Royal Society for the Protection of Birds and the British Trust for Ornithology.

After consulting with the Prime Minister, the Home Secretary issued a terse broadcast over all BBC television and radio stations, every thirty minutes, stating that Her Majesty's Government was investigating and monitoring the incident and coordinating closely with the relevant authorities in France, Germany, and Ireland; that the flocks of migrating birds had been observed on multiple occasions taking proactive steps to avoid flying into any airborne planes or stationary structures and to avoid injury to humans or damage to property; and that, until the Government issued new instructions and more could be learned about the birds' intentions, under no circumstances should any of the birds be shot or otherwise interfered with unless absolutely necessary to defend against an unprovoked avian attack. The Home Secretary concluded by stating that the Government would provide further updates as new information became available and gave out a toll-free telephone number for citizens to make reports or seek assistance.

At Animal Farm, the farmhouse phone had rung several times since the pigs and humans had sat down for lunch just before noon. But the pigs, having just shipped in several cases of a new and highly-touted India Pale Ale from Newcastle, were too busy swilling it down and refilling their beer glasses to bother answering it.

A few minutes before two o'clock, a young farmhand who had finished his lunch earlier than the others was walking a little unsteadily toward the cow pasture a hundred or so yards from the farmhouse. He heard a rising clatter of hooves hitting the ground behind him to his left, followed quickly by a vision of rapid movement obscured by clouds of dirt and dust. He stopped in his tracks. Scores of farm animals–horses, sheep, donkeys, cows, goats, geese, and even a few cats and hens–were running or galloping at full speed toward the boundary fence next to the turnip field. Between the horses and donkeys and, twenty yards to the rear, the sheep, goats, cows, geese, cats, and hens, there appeared, further back and at grass level, an irregular black swath about three yards wide whose leading edge was also moving slowly but inexorably in the same direction and which, the farmhand concluded to his horror, was a long, marching column of ants, beetles, spiders, and other insects.

The sinister column of marching insects having taken away his powers of intelligible speech, the best the terrified farmhand could manage was to yell out at the top of his lungs, "Holy Shit! *Holy Shit!*," and scramble back to the farmhouse. Panting for breath, he reached the porch just as Napoleon stumbled out of the doorway, followed by the pigs and the farmhands.

A raucous din of squawking and cawing birds caused them all to look skyward. Thousands of ravens, crows, blackbirds, magpies, and pigeons were meticulously perching themselves on the tree branches, roofs, and hedgerows and along all the power lines and the adjoining farms, as far as the eye could see, while a vast, undulating black cloud of birds appeared on the horizon and blotted out the sun. As the afternoon sky darkened ominously, Napoleon could just make out the animals from his own farm, and from Pilkington's and Frederick's farms, running toward the boundary fences and massing alongside them.

The farm's shotguns were kept in a locked tool-shed just behind the farmhouse. Napoleon shouted at the farmhands to get them and then shouted for his guard dogs. But the pack of vicious dogs that rarely left Napoleon's side could be seen racing out the main gate and down the county road, with nary a backward glance by any of them.

Meanwhile, a flock of birds had broken off from the approaching black cloud and was heading straight for the farmhouse. With an audience of thousands, perhaps tens of thousands, of other birds now perched on all of the adjacent power lines and tree branches and silently watching their every move, the birds that had broken formation circled the farmhouse and descended with military precision. Some of them alighted on the roofs of the farmhouse, the toolshed, the big barn, the cowshed, and the other farm buildings. The rest of them landed on patches of open ground near the farmhouse and the adjacent pastures, being

careful to leave a skirt of ground around the farmhouse and a narrow lane between the farmhouse
and the toolshed.

The birds who had formed the huge black cloud
had now landed and all of the fields and pastures
of Animal Farm, Pilkington's farm, and Frederick's
farm were blanketed, in the tens of thousands,
by ravens, crows, blackbirds, magpies, pigeons,
house sparrows, pied wagtails, blue tits, starlings,
great tits, chaffinches, arctic terns, collared doves,
robins, lapwings, golden plovers, swallows, dun-
nocks, whooper swans, redwings, goldfinches,
swifts, Greenland white fronted geese, Canada
geese, corncrakes, shelducks, ospreys, ruffs, roll-
ers, spotted eagles, cranes, bar-tailed godwits,
barnacle geese, wallcreepers, siskins, black-
necked grebes, marlins, larks, wrens, Egyptian
vultures, song thrushes, sanderlings, kingfishers,
and collared pratincoles.

As the bewildered group of seven farmhands
ran frantically back to the farmhouse porch, shotguns in hand, Snowball (with Moses standing stiffly
and somewhat ceremoniously on Snowball's right
shoulder), Clover, and Benjamin appeared from
behind the farmhouse and stood in front of the
porch while hundreds of groundling ravens and
other birds pressed around them. Moses hopped
to the ground and stood to Snowball's right. Clover
made her way over to Snowball's left, moving gingerly to avoid trampling any of the birds. Benjamin
remained in his place, a few feet behind the other

three. The animals who had massed along the boundary fences, and all of the birds on the ground and in the trees and roofs and along the power lines, looked on avidly but made no sound.

Napoleon, his sweaty snout twitching profusely as he tried to stare down the rebels, was momentarily distracted by a sensation of warm urine trickling down the insides of his hind legs and making little yellow puddles beneath him. For the first time since the Battle of the Cowshed many years before, Napoleon had wet himself.

Snowball noticed the puddles of urine ebbing at Napoleon's feet, shook his head in mingled triumph and disgust, and stepped forward with confidence.

"Napoleon, as everyone can see, your reports of my death were greatly exaggerated. I will not mince words with you. We are taking back Animal Farm. We hope to do so peaceably. If that is not possible, we are prepared to fight, and to die, if necessary–and in that event, we are consoled by the fact that you, too, along with your pig and human friends, are also certain to die. And if you think you can kill all of us before that happens, you are welcome to try. But I would advise against it. Look around you. All it will take is one signal from me and you and the other pigs and humans will be eaten alive by the birds. When they are finished with you, not even your bones will be left for burial."

Snowball reached for a piece of the broken leather whip he had discovered in the barn a few nights before, which Clover had carried in her teeth for today's occasion and had just dropped at his feet. Snowball placed the whip between the knuckles of his trotter, stood up on his hind legs, and held the whip up to Napoleon and then swung it around so that the birds and the other animals could see it. The birds on the roof and in the trees and along the power lines fluttered and cawed aggressively but made no overtly threatening gesture.

"Here is one of your whips, Napoleon. Fittingly, I have broken it in two. It symbolizes the terror and despotism you and your pig enablers have inflicted on the citizens of Animal Farm. If I toss this whip in the air, that will signal the bird and animal comrades to attack. As the humans sometimes say, 'It's showtime.' You and your men have ten seconds to throw down your guns and escape with your lives. The ten seconds start *now*."

Napoleon, vastly overmatched and a coward at heart, didn't need ten seconds. After quickly ordering the humans to put down their guns, he turned to Snowball. "I expect safe passage for me and the others."

"Not so fast," Snowball replied curtly. "We want all of the farm keys, all of the cash on hand, all of the bank checks and bank account records, the title deeds to Animal Farm, the title documents for all of the farm vehicles and equipment, and your credit and debit cards. When we have all of those, you will be permitted to leave. Of course, the guns stay here. And just to get rid of you as quickly as possible, we'll let you leave with the old truck that the humans use for loading manure. The rest of the farm vehicles stay here. I said that you will escape with your lives. That is all you will escape with. Moses, please take a contingent of your most alert and vigilant crow and raven comrades and accompany Napoleon and the others while they collect what is ours. None of them is to make or receive any phone calls. If any of them tries that or offers any resistance, you are authorized to use all necessary force."

Moses and about a hundred crow and raven volunteers accompanied Napoleon and his group as they re-entered the farmhouse to collect the items Snowball had demanded. The horses, cows, goats, chickens, geese, cats, donkeys, and sheep who had massed along the inner boundary fences ambled back to the vicinity of the farmhouse and, like a silent Greek chorus, waited anxiously for the rest of the afternoon's drama to unfold.

A few minutes later, Moses came out again and hopped over to where Snowball, Clover, and Benjamin were standing and then fluttered onto Benjamin's back.

"Is everything under control?" Snowball asked Moses.

"Yes, Snowball. Everything on your list is being gathered and the pigs and humans are cooperating. Do you have a moment? The four of us need to talk."

"Yes," Snowball replied. "I haven't had a chance to ask you how you got so many birds to show up on such short notice and from such faraway places. The birds really came through for you, Moses, and for *us*. We are in your debt."

"You are most welcome, Snowball. That's what I wanted to talk to you about. I had to make some promises to the birds–promises that might complicate things a bit."

"What promises?"

Moses looked away nervously. "Promises about what you would try to do for them if our strategy worked today and if the human authorities get involved."

"I don't understand, Moses," Snowball replied.

"I'm afraid I don't either," Clover added. "Please explain."

"Okay. When I approached the local birds early Tuesday morning, they told their friends, and then their friends told *their* friends, and so on. Within twenty-four hours, I had solid pledges of support not only from our bird comrades in Sussex, Kent, Surrey, and Hampshire but also from Devon and Cornwall and from across the Irish Sea and the English Channel. Somehow, and unbeknownst to me, the birds here and across the waters got together and decided that, as a condition of their support, we would use the leverage created by the mass bird migrations to get the British Government to persuade other governments to set up animal-led communities in their countries too. The initial list of countries mentioned by the birds included the Republic of Ireland, France, and Germany. But then some of the more militant Irish and French birds insisted that, given how many close relatives they have in Canada and the United States, those countries need to be added to the list."

"Why wasn't I told about this before?" Snowball demanded.

Moses was unrepentant. "Snowball, you told us in no uncertain terms that unless enough birds showed up today, your plan was doomed. I took you strictly at your word. Look around you. I think it's fair to say that enough birds showed up today. We are on the verge of taking back the farm only because tens of thousands of birds answered your call. We need to repay that debt. If we get to negotiate terms with the humans but fail to achieve the outcomes the birds want, I will explain that to them and they will accept my explanation. And whatever else happens, the birds will have helped us retake the farm and we aren't giving it back. You mentioned the game of poker a few nights ago and I've been reading up on it. It seems to me that, right now, we're 'playing with house money.'"

Snowball paused to reflect on the surprising news Moses had conveyed and then replied crisply. "Okay, let's stay focused. We need to get the pigs and the humans squared away and out of here. After that, you, Clover, Benjamin, and I can figure out what to do with the birds."

By three o'clock, Napoleon and his group of frightened, disconsolate pigs and farmhands had handed over all the keys, money, documents, and credit cards to Snowball and were ready to depart Animal Farm. After taking care to ask Snowball's permission, a young farmhand started up the manure truck. Napoleon seated himself in the front seat while the rest of the pigs and humans crowded into the back of the truck, closed the tail-gate, and defended their nostrils against the pungent smell of fresh manure. With a few dozen ravens standing on the truck's hood and on its roof and front and back bumpers, a farmhand drove the truck and its shell-shocked passengers through the main gate. After the farmhand closed the five-barred gate behind him and the truck drove away, the raven escorts flew back to the farmhouse and were greeted by loud cheers and wild applause.

"Comrades," Snowball shouted out triumphantly. "Today's victory is yours alone. Thanks to your courage and grit, we have succeeded in taking back our farm. There is much to discuss and many plans to make. The birds have requested that we speak to the humans about setting up other animal-led communities. I am not sure how to accomplish that but we will try. Take the rest of the afternoon to celebrate and tonight we'll meet and begin planning our future. I know some of you will be tempted, but please do not destroy any of the pigs' or humans' property—we may find a use for it, if only to trade it for other items the farm needs. And finally, we ask that all of the visiting birds here and on the neighboring farms not depart until after tonight's meeting. Congratulations! You are now working only for *yourselves* and not for pigs or humans."

The animals could hardly believe their good fortune. They had taken back their farm and no two-legged, four-legged, multilegged, or winged creature had been injured or shot in the process.

And Napoleon–who, only hours before, had been the fearful, invulnerable, larger-than-life tyrant whose every whim and cruelty had to be accepted without question or protest–had been defrocked as a traitor and a coward and unceremoniously sent packing.

After Snowball offered his congratulations and completed his remarks, the birds on the ground and in the trees and on the power lines flew up into the air and wheeled and circled joyously, a whirring cyclone of wings, beaks, and tails. The horses, goats, sheep, donkeys, cows, chickens, cats, and hens–walking, running, or galloping after their fashion–made three full circuits of the boundaries of the farm before settling down to graze in the fields or rest in the shade of one of the farm's ancient oak trees. The farm's insects mostly made themselves scarce, underground or in trees or hedges, to avoid being trampled in all the commotion. And though many of the birds and animals were sorely tempted to enter the farmhouse and toolshed and destroy any item used by a pig or a human, they resisted that temptation in deference to Snowball's request.

As the other animals were celebrating, Clover, Moses, Benjamin, and Snowball found a quiet spot behind the toolshed and resumed their discussion about what to do about the birds and their extraordinary request.

Moses, initially uncertain about the best way to re-engage Snowball on the question, decided that full transparency was a good place to start.

"Snowball, Clover, and Benjamin, there is another piece of information you should be aware of. Three nights ago, after you were all asleep, some of the raven elders visited me and asked what they and the other birds should say if the humans tried to communicate with them while they were en route to Animal Farm. With so many birds in flight, many of us thought it likely that humans from the Home Office or the Ministry of Defense or from one of the bird protection groups would seek us out and ask our intentions."

"That makes sense," Snowball replied. "What did you come up with?"

"Recognizing," Moses continued, "that the birds hoped to engage the humans in a larger conversation, the best I could come up with was to tell the birds just to shout out to the humans: *'Snowball knows! Remember the Birds! Long Live Animal Farm!'*"

Snowball had a good idea why Moses had given that instruction. "Your idea was to drop my name, and Animal Farm's name, so the humans would know whom to deal with and where to find him, right?"

"Right."

"And you threw in the '*Remember the Birds!*' piece just to remind the humans what the birds are capable of, if provoked, and if they all band together to defend themselves?"

"Exactly right."

Snowball glanced over at Clover and Benjamin. "Moses, I wish you had consulted us before issuing those instructions. You've put us and the rest of the animals in a tough spot. With all of the work that needs to be done to get the farm back on its feet and functioning as a true collective, I don't see how we can engage with the humans on these larger issues, at least right now. Clover, Benjamin, what do you think?"

"Snowball, I agree that Moses's action, though well-intentioned, was rash," Clover replied. "But one thing is certain. Someone high up in the British Government will be calling on us, and soon. The bird migrations over the past couple of days have made national *and* international news and this incident has even sparked emergency radio and television broadcasts from the BBC. As long as our bird comrades remain a visible presence and don't provoke a human military response, don't we still hold a very strong hand? And to take your poker example a little further, aren't we well-positioned to bluff the humans into granting the birds' requests? The cards we hold now, it seems to me, are as strong as they ever will be, at least in our lifetimes. Maybe we should play this hand out."

Before Snowball could respond to Clover, or to Benjamin's enthusiastic nods in agreement to the points Clover had just made, a young raven fluttered overhead and alighted expertly on Benjamin's shoulder.

"Apologies, everyone, for interrupting, but I thought you should know," the raven said. "Six large black vans just turned into the farm and are driving up the main road, as we speak. Each van has a large seal on its front doors and on the roof."

"What is your name, comrade?" Clover asked.

"Oisin," the young raven answered.

"Thank you, Oisin. Could you make out the writing on the vans?"

Oisin nodded excitedly. "The writing says, Secretary of State for the Home Department, Her Majesty's Government of the United Kingdom."

CHAPTER 3

Snowball trotted to the back corner of the tool-shed and, after confirming Oisin's report, returned to the anxious group.

"We'll have to think and act fast," Snowball told them. "Clover, Benjamin, Moses, do I have your authority to 'play this hand out' with the humans and try to get us and the birds the best deal I can? There is no time to explain. I need to know right now."

Snowball's three comrades nodded their approval.

"Alright," Snowball continued, "just follow my lead and let *me* do the talking. Moses, I need you and Oisin–"

Oisin cut him off. "Snowball, you should know that I represented the Cornish birds when we told Moses the price of our participation. So you'll need *my* proxy too."

Snowball gave the young raven an icy stare. "Do I have it?"

Oisin turned to Moses. "Moses, do I have your word that Snowball can be trusted and will not sell us out?"

"Absolutely. Snowball will keep his word," Moses replied.

"Yes, I will," Snowball added. "So what will it be? Time is short."

"You have the birds' proxy," Oisin said. "Tell us what you want us to do."

"Good," Snowball continued, speaking more quickly now. "We need to show the humans strength, but also coolness and discipline. Moses and Oisin, go tell the ravens that we'll need small flocks of them to land on the hoods and roofs of the humans' vans in an orderly way, but *not* on the windshields or windows. As soon as I come onto the front porch of the farmhouse and raise my trotter, they should fly off the vans and land close by, wherever they can find a tree branch or a patch of open ground– and they should make no threatening gesture to the humans, *whatever* the humans do. Go!"

As each of the six, tightly-spaced black vans rolled to a stop on the farmhouse's unpaved circular driveway and before any of the vans' occupants had a chance to get out, three hundred ravens launched themselves from their various perches and alighted on each van, precisely as Snowball had directed. The front passenger door of the first van opened a few inches and then closed quickly, before any raven had a chance to enter the passenger compartment.

Meanwhile, Snowball, Clover, and Benjamin made their way through the back door of the farmhouse and into the small foyer just inside the door that led to the front porch. Snowball directed Clover and Benjamin to stand behind him when they reached the porch and to let *him* do the talking.

Snowball opened the front door and stepped onto the porch, with Clover and Benjamin close behind him.

The windshields and windows of each black van were heavily tinted. Snowball could not make out any of the occupants' faces but did detect muddled signs of movement in the front and back seats and knew that he was being watched closely.

After peering through each tinted windshield and window, Snowball conspicuously raised his right front trotter and the ravens flew up from the hoods and roofs of the vans and landed where they could.

Thirty seconds later, the front passenger door of the first van opened and discharged a stocky, thirtyish man wearing a dark blue suit and sunglasses. Snowball eyed him closely and surmised that the bulge inside the man's suit jacket was a gun of some sort. The man returned Snowball's stare and then opened the rear passenger door. Two men got out–unarmed, as far as Snowball could tell. The taller of the two men was in his early sixties, tanned and distinguished-looking, and wore a charcoal gray suit of expensive cut. The other man was also presentably dressed, but much younger. Once both men had exited the van, the man with the bulge in his suit unbuttoned his jacket, closed the front and back passenger doors and stood facing the porch, his right hand and wrist obscured by his jacket.

The taller man paused to take in the astonishing scene of thousands of birds and a smattering of farm animals massed in every direction, motionless and staring at him intently. Recovering his nerve somewhat, he walked up to the front porch where Snowball was standing. "I am Sir Ambrose Dinsdale, Home Secretary of the Government of the United Kingdom. This is my chief of staff, Anthony Richards-Steele. I take it you are Snowball?"

"That's right," Snowball answered. "Let me introduce my comrades, Clover and Benjamin."

"Pleased to meet you. Is there somewhere we can talk privately?"

"We can talk here," Snowball replied, motioning to two old but serviceable wicker chairs in the corner of the porch. "I represent the birds and farm animals in this matter and have nothing to hide from them."

"Very well," Dinsdale said, taking one of the offered chairs as his chief of staff pulled the other chair closer and took out a pen and a notebook. "Her Majesty's Government wishes to know your intentions. You and your colleagues have caused quite a stir in the past twenty-four hours, not just in England, and have frightened quite a lot of people. The Prime Minister requested that I come here straight away and report back to him and to the rest of the Cabinet."

"As we have shown by our conduct, our intentions are peaceful," Snowball said. "We have taken back our farm from the pigs who were running it and who were starving, mistreating, and murdering the other farm animals. I note that the pigs' cruelty was enabled by humans and that 'Her Majesty's Government' did nothing to stop it. We have no intention of giving the farm back. By my estimate, upwards of a hundred thousand birds have shown up in the past day or so in support of our bloodless insurrection. On my express instructions, the birds and the other animals have acted peaceably. It is their fervent wish, as it is my wish, to live in peace with the humans and with their governments. We have very reasonable demands and would be happy to share them if your Government thinks that would be productive."

"And if we do *not* think that would be productive?" Dinsdale asked.

"In that event," Snowball answered coolly, "I cannot guarantee that the tens of thousands of birds who flew here yesterday and today and the three hundred-odd *billion* birds elsewhere on the planet–leaving aside the countless other wild animals who are committed to our cause, in the United Kingdom and elsewhere–will think it in their interests to continue conducting themselves so peaceably."

Upon hearing Snowball's answer, the birds on the ground nearest the porch and along the power lines and hedges closest to the farmhouse began cawing and screeching at almost deafening volume, prompting all of the nearby horses, cows, sheep, hens, geese, and other farm animals to do the same. The outburst was not in Snowball's script, but its passion and spontaneity warmed him and he made no move to stop it. Dinsdale stood up briskly and motioned the men and women in his security detail–who, on hearing the commotion, had exited their vans and drawn their handguns–to stand down and get back into the vans. Dinsdale's chief of staff, visibly shaken, dropped his pen and, after three clumsy attempts, managed to pick it up again. A moment later, all was quiet.

Dinsdale sat down, wiped his brow with his handkerchief, and leaned forward. "Snowball, what exactly *are* your demands?"

"First, a binding, perpetual commitment that neither the British Government nor any local government will interfere with our running the farm for the benefit of all the animals and will protect the farm against human interference. Second, that your Government work to persuade its counterparts in Ireland, France, Germany, Canada, and the United States to establish comparable animal-led communities in each of those countries. We do recognize that this second demand is not entirely within your control but we expect an aggressive and ultimately successful diplomatic effort. And the birds and animals I represent have other levers we can pull, here and elsewhere, if the negotiations do not proceed with urgency."

Dinsdale shifted nervously in his chair. "Just so I am clear and can report back to the Prime Minister, the other 'levers' to which you refer would involve demonstrations of massed animal resistance, such as the one occurring now?"

"No," Snowball answered crisply, "not like this one. *This* demonstration was designed to show humans how frightening, but also how disciplined and orderly, the birds and animals can be. I trust you are a student of history. Today's demonstration is like the leaflets the Americans dropped on Hiroshima and Nagasaki before dropping the hydrogen bombs, to warn Japanese civilians of the imminent terror and to give them a chance to flee the danger or sue for peace. Our next demonstration, whatever form it takes, won't be like the leaflets episode. It will be more like what happened at Hiroshima and Nagasaki after the Japanese ignored the leaflets."

Richards-Steele, who was taking copious long-hand notes of the conversation, added an extraneous note in brackets [See Daphne du Maurier's story, The Birds–except this time it's real and the birds will negotiate before attacking.]

"You've made yourself very clear, Snowball," Dinsdale responded. "I will report back to the Prime Minister and the Cabinet directly. I take it I can represent to the PM and to the leaders of the other governments that you and your colleagues will take no aggressive or irrevocable step, here or elsewhere, until the negotiations you seek are concluded? I will need to make that representation and be able to convince my Government that it will be honored."

"Let me put it this way, Sir Ambrose," Snowball said. "The birds and animals I represent will take no irrevocable step, assuming the humans do likewise–and that includes humans who live in the United Kingdom but are not part of the Government. The birds, in particular, are through with being shot at for sport, caged for amusement, tarred with oil and grease after tanker spills, and watching their natural habitats destroyed by human folly. In the past few days, the birds have come to realize the power they wield if they all band together and act with a single purpose. That genie is now out of the bottle and I won't answer for their conduct if the humans try any sort of unprovoked military response. If anyone tries that, you will have a bloody mess on your hands–not to mention the political repercussions for you and your governing party in Parliament. So I leave you with one thought: *Remember the Birds!*"

"I do understand, Snowball. Let me get back to London and make my report. I trust you will make yourself available by phone?"

"Yes."

"Then good day to you. I'll be in touch very soon."

Dinsdale nodded to the man with the bulge in his jacket, who opened the rear passenger door of the van. After the three men were safely in, the van moved slowly down the entrance road, followed closely by the five other vans.

Once the vans had reached the county road

just beyond the main gate, Clover bent her head down and gave Snowball a gentle nudge. "Well done, Snowball. We are all proud of you. Major and Boxer would be proud of you too."

Moses and Oisin, who had watched the proceedings from a ringside perch on the eaves of the toolshed, flew over to the group and alighted on Benjamin's back.

Snowball turned to address them. "Thank you, Clover. And thank you, Benjamin, Moses, and Oisin, for your support today. I did my best. And as I was talking to Dinsdale, it did strike me how much all this does resemble a poker game. I hope I didn't overplay my hand. We shall see."

Upon receiving the Home Secretary's report, the Prime Minister and other Cabinet members expressed a wide range of strongly held, and often flatly contradictory, views. The Minister of Defense argued that anything less than a robust military response to the animals' veiled threats would constitute "appeasement" and suggested, as an essential first step, that industrial-scale bird nets be installed around the Houses of Parliament, Whitehall, and other key government buildings and military installations. The Foreign Secretary, supported by Dinsdale, vehemently disagreed and urged a diplomatic solution that would reduce the likelihood of hostilities and enable each side to save face and claim victory. The Minister of Defense countered by insisting that no foreign government be approached or briefed until the domestic defense strategy of Her Majesty's Government was in place. The Foreign Secretary again begged to differ and urged immediate outreach to the Governments of Ireland, France, Germany, Canada, and the United States so that information could be shared and multilateral negotiations promptly commenced.

The Lord Chancellor and Secretary of State for Justice, an octogenarian from the West Midlands, took an entirely different tack and warned of the grave consequences that might ensue from encouraging birds and other wild animals to entertain "ideas above their station," including destruction of time-honored British customs dating back centuries. "What, is there to be no more *falconry?*" he exclaimed. "No more *riding to hounds?* No more *annual grouse shoots on the Yorkshire moors?*"

After an occasionally heated debate (and after giving due deference to the eccentric views expressed by The Right Honorable Gentleman from Birmingham), the Prime Minister told the Cabinet that he was inclined to agree with the Foreign and Home Secretaries. He would personally brief the Queen, the leader of Her Majesty's Loyal Opposition, and the leaders of Ireland, France, Germany, Canada, and the United States, after which the Foreign Secretary would follow up with her counterparts in each of those five nations. The PM asked the Home Secretary to reach out to Snowball and tell him that multilateral discussions were expected to commence shortly and that he would keep Snowball quietly informed. Dinsdale was also authorized to assure Snowball that Her Majesty's Government would make a binding legal commitment, formalized by an Act of Parliament, that the animals' group ownership of the farm would be protected in perpetuity. Each Cabinet member was directed to consult with his or her senior advisors, get them fully briefed, and start working on contingency plans if the plan faltered or hostilities erupted.

Finally, the PM–who had read Moderns at Cambridge and was a voracious reader of literary fiction (even, as his Cabinet colleagues sometimes ribbed him, during Question Time in the House of Commons)–gave each Cabinet member a more unconventional homework assignment, which he strongly urged them to share with their Parliamentary Under Secretaries and other key government colleagues: namely, to read, at their very earliest convenience, Daphne du Maurier's short story, *The Birds* and, after that, to watch Alfred Hitchcock's feature film based on that story. He directed the Cabinet Secretary to distribute copies of du Maurier's piece and to arrange for private evening showings of the Hitchcock film in the House of Commons Library.

The marathon Cabinet meeting ran into the wee hours and Dinsdale decided to wait until the next morning to call Snowball and brief him on the Government's proposed plan of action.

Snowball relayed the news to Clover, Benjamin, Moses, and Oisin and requested that they join him right away to talk strategy. Snowball posed to his colleagues the key decisions now confronting them: while the British Government was negotiating for the creation of animal-led communities in each of the five named countries, should the birds that had made their extraordinary migrations remain in the area to confirm their solidarity and support for the animals' cause? Alternatively, should the birds return from whence they came, as a gesture of the animals' good faith and willingness to let the human diplomatic processes play out? Was there a viable third option that would enhance the likelihood of a successful outcome?

Moses and Oisin argued that the birds should remain in place and that their wholesale departures, at this early and inconclusive stage, would signal weakness and lack of resolve. Snowball acknowledged the point but thought that the birds' continued presence in and around Animal Farm, in vast numbers and perhaps for many more weeks or even months, would dramatically increase the chance that some disgruntled human or group of humans unaffiliated with the Government would get "spooked," fire shots at the birds, and trigger an altercation that would make further negotiations untenable. Clover and Benjamin deferred to Snowball, given his successful strategy and tactics so far. It was finally agreed that the birds should return to their places of origin–not all at once, but in a measured, orderly way over the next week to ten days–and that the birds reserved the right to "send a message" to the humans if the negotiations dragged out.

Representatives from the United Kingdom, the United States, Canada, Ireland, France, and Germany agreed to meet in Reykjavik, Iceland, to discuss the birds' demands. Although each country had its own unique challenges to establishing an animal-led community within its borders, on one point they were substantially agreed: none of them had any appetite for a potentially catastrophic confrontation with legions of birds and other wild animals. The Foreign Ministers from Canada and Ireland took special pains to point out that, given the small human populations in Canada and Ireland relative to the vastly greater number of birds that resided there, the birds' numerical superiority would, in any confrontation with the humans, result in a bloodbath. The Governments of France and Germany were also supportive and had taken discreet steps to identify tracts of farmland that could be transferred to animal control in the manner least disruptive and expensive.

The United States, however, opposed the plan in principle and, according to leaked reports from the early Reykjavik meetings, its representatives had become querulous and unaccommodating. A wild rumor circulated that the U.S. Department of Defense was developing a nerve gas that was deadly to birds but harmless to humans, which Department officials categorically denied. Issues of border security, a common currency, and the vexed question whether a nonhuman born in a U.S.-sanctioned animal community within the territory of the United States would, under the U.S. Constitution, become a "citizen of the United States" also gave the Americans pause. The Foreign Ministers of the five other countries reminded the American Secretary of State that unless all of the participating countries agreed to the birds' demands, the safety of humans in each of those countries, including in the United States, could be at risk.

As the negotiations dragged out and as Sir Ambrose Dinsdale's back-channel reports to Snowball became daily more pessimistic, Moses and Oisin approached Snowball and argued that it was time to "send a message" to the humans. Snowball agreed.

At dawn the next morning, the offshore waters of some of the busiest ports in North America and Western Europe–New York, Los Angeles, Long Beach, Houston, Seattle, Vancouver, Montreal, Halifax, Hamburg, Bremerhaven, Le Havre, Marseille, Dunkirk, London, Liverpool, Southampton, Felixstowe, Cardiff, Dublin, and Cork–witnessed scenes which, as *The Times of London* wrote on its front page, above the fold, "were frighteningly reminiscent of Daphne du Maurier's short story, *The Birds*: Hundreds, thousands, tens of thousands of gulls rose and fell in the trough of the seas, heads to the wind, like a mighty fleet at anchor, waiting on the tide and stretching as far as the eye could see, in close formation, line upon line."

In a special Page One editorial, the *Times* expressed its hope that the gulls' ominous displays of life imitating art would cause humans and their governments to reflect more deeply on how to live on better terms with the planet's other species.

Later that day, the citizens of London, Berlin, Paris, Dublin, Ottawa, and Washington, D.C., experienced another unprecedented sight: in each city, during the busy luncheon hour, huge sky banners were observed circling the skyline–pulled, not by airplanes, but by flocks of fiercely squawking crows and ravens tethered to each end of the banner.

Each banner proclaimed, in bold red letters, "Remember the Birds!"

Following the international hubbub created by these two extraordinary events, the Reykjavik negotiations proceeded with renewed vigor and Snowball and his colleagues concluded that the birds' message had been duly received.

A week later, at a press conference covered by print, television, and digital media outlets from around the world and at which Snowball, Moses, and Oisin featured prominently (Clover had contracted bronchitis and had remained in England, with Benjamin by her side), it was announced that although many details remained to be worked out, the Governments of the United Kingdom, Ireland, France, Germany, Canada, and the United States had agreed to establish within their respective borders communities governed solely by the animals who resided there and whose status as sovereign nations would be internationally respected.

The British Foreign Secretary announced that, in the spirit of the fresh start and improved fellowship the human and nonhuman species hoped to foster, the animal community in Sussex, England, would henceforth be known as the Albion Creature Community. In response to a question from *The Guardian*, the Foreign Minister made clear that birds and animals born in Scotland, Wales, and Northern Ireland, in addition to those born in England, would be presumptively eligible for Albion citizenship.

The American Secretary of State declared that the animal community established in the United States, whose size and location were still under discussion, would be called the United State of Animals but, to avoid confusion, would be referenced in maps and other official government documents as Animal Farm USA.

Within weeks of these announcements, statements issued by the Russian Federation, the People's Republic of China, and the Republic of Mexico confirmed that animal-led communities would also be established in those countries; that working groups of human and animal representatives in each country were meeting privately to discuss the location and size of each community; and that more Information would be forthcoming shortly. Soon after the Chinese announcement, the Dalai Lama announced that Tibet would also establish a sovereign animal community so that birds and animals who wished to live in a community inspired by Buddhist teachings would have an alternative to the one established by China.

Three nights later, Snowball died peacefully in his sleep. Given his founding role in the so-called Creature Insurrection (a term coined by *The Guardian*), Snowball's death was covered widely in the news media. As his body lay in state at the farmhouse, dignitaries from each of the eight countries that had agreed to establish animal-led communities visited Albion to eulogize Snowball and proclaim a new era in inter-species cooperation and coexistence. Snowball was granted the posthumous title of Albion's Founding Father and was laid to rest at the foot of the orchard beside Major's grave.

Oisin was elected to lead Albion going forward and promised, with the continued wise counsel of Clover, Moses, and Benjamin, to build on Snowball's remarkable legacy. In his first official acts, and after consulting with focus groups drawn from a cross-section of Albion's bird and animal citizenry, Oisin announced that Albion's national flag would be two pieces of a broken human whip superimposed on a simple background of pasture green; and that he would meet, as soon as practicable, with leaders from the other newly-established animal nations to set up a worldwide advocacy organization, the International Congress of Free

Animals, which would include representation of whales, dolphins, fishes, and other marine life.

No one at Albion had any information about Napoleon or his whereabouts–but a visiting purple-necked ostrich from Devon reported that she had seen a pig matching Napoleon's description wearing a tattered black-and-white-striped bathrobe and pacing the garden paths at an inebriates' home in Plymouth.

In the aftermath of the creation of animal communities in each sponsoring country, human and animal leaders arrived over time at a set of core understandings about how the different species would co-exist. Although those mutual understandings varied from country to country (for example, the Russian Foreign Minister stated that his country would honor the animals' choice of a form of government, provided that Joseph Stalin's enduring legacy was duly respected), they followed the same general pattern.

The animals would be left to govern themselves but would be expected to protect the safety and property of humans who visited or had business there. The humans would take no step to prevent birds or animals from relocating to the animal community within their country's borders but, on the other hand, the leaders of each animal community would be responsible for ensuring that conditions there did not pose a health hazard to adjacent human populations. The humans would develop no chemical warfare or other military means designed to injure or kill only nonhuman animal species and, in turn, the leaders in each animal community would take all necessary steps to prevent mass bird and animal attacks on humans or their property.

The raising and eventual slaughter of animals outside of each animal community would be more tightly regulated by the humans, with a view to promoting more humane treatment of farm animals and an eventual reduction in the quantity of birds, animals, and fish consumed by humans. Game animals that were not endangered species and did not live in an animal community could still be hunted for sport by humans but each human government would more closely monitor this practice and take steps to encourage its eventual abandonment.

In consideration for the humans' agreement to share technologies that would enable animal communities to increase their crop yields and communicate more easily with their counterparts in other countries, the animals would share their unique insights on animal husbandry and veterinary science. The birds, in particular, would provide the humans with information and insights on the nature and extent of changes in the earth's atmosphere and their effects on bird and animal habitats and, reciprocally, the humans would aggressively step up their efforts to reduce greenhouse gas emissions and the levels of carbon dioxide in the atmosphere.

In one of the most significant developments of

the post-Creature-Insurrection period, a great blue heron from High Park in Toronto came up with the idea of creating and disseminating posters with the theme, *Remember the Birds!* The most popular version featured two, sharply contrasting scenes: in the upper left, a bucolic scene of birds singing and playing with gleeful young children and their parents at a backyard human picnic; in the bottom right, separated by a thin diagonal dotted line, a terrifying image of flocks of birds mercilessly pecking the heads and eyes of human children on their way home from school. Animal rights and bird protection groups in the Americas, Europe, and Asia amplified the message by creating their own high-quality posters, images from which soon began to appear on urban and highway billboards; on the sides of buses and inside the subway stations and subway cars in New York, Washington, D.C., Mexico City, Toronto, Montreal, London, Paris, Berlin, Rome, Tokyo, Beijing, and Moscow; and as full-page spreads in the world's largest-circulation newspapers and magazines.

The billboard and advertising program proved highly effective in driving home to humans and their governments that, if push came to shove, they would be hard-pressed to defend themselves against a coordinated, worldwide bird and animal insurrection and should conduct themselves accordingly.

In the ensuing years and decades, and with progressively increasing exchanges between members of the animal and human communities, citizens of Animal Farm USA, Albion, and the other animal nations in North America and Europe began to exhibit some of the quirks and enthusiasms of the human populations that enveloped them.

At Animal Farm USA, the animals tended to be more individualistic and entrepreneurial, more schooled in the ways of business, and surprisingly passionate about the competitive fates of professional sports teams, particularly baseball, basketball, and football (although, given the newfound availability of specially-designed golf clubs and tennis rackets for four-legged creatures, interest in golf and tennis was also gaining ground.)

North of the 49th parallel, in Beaverville, the animals trended moderately socialist and strongly internationalist in outlook and many had learned to skate on frozen ponds and to play ice hockey (using a piece of frozen horse or cow turd as a puck, if a real puck wasn't to hand and, in the beavers' case, using their tails as hockey sticks.)

At the Albion Creature Community in Sussex, England, a surprising number of birds and animals had become versed in Shakespeare and Milton and exhibited fierce tribal loyalties to various soccer teams in the English Premier League.

The animal and bird citizens of Place des Animaux, in the south of France, had taken to weaning their offspring on red wine mixed with water and were more tolerant on issues of marital infidelity and sexual mores.

At Sovietski Farm in Russia, the centuries-old hardships suffered by the average Russian, human and nonhuman–first under the czars, then under Bolshevik and communist rule and, more recently, under an authoritarian kleptocracy–had caused the animals to be guarded, wary, nationalistic, and military-minded and also openly envious of the freedoms and living standards that had been achieved in the more democratic West. (The animal citizens of Sovietski Farm were also extraordinarily creative and accomplished in other areas, including in the performing arts. Humans fortunate enough to witness a Sovietski Farm performance of Tchaikovsky's Swan Lake with actual swans in the title roles and in the corps de ballet, accompanied by a 106-member all-animal symphony orchestra that rivaled the Berlin Philharmonic in tonal beauty and precision of attack, all agreed that it was an unforgettable, even life-changing, experience.)

The cross-pollination of animal and human cultures led, over time, to diversity initiatives that would have astonished Major and Snowball.

Former presidents and other prominent citizens of Animal Farm USA, Beaverville, Albion, Place des Animaux, and Land der Deutschen Kreaturen in Germany now sat on the boards of influential human nonprofit organizations in the United States, Canada, Mexico, England, France, and Germany, and on the boards of long-established for-profit companies with iconic brands. A West Highland White Terrier had recently been elected Chair of the Board of Trustees of the American Federation of Humane Societies; a 65-year-old gopher tortoise sat on the audit committee of the World Wildlife Fund; a former champion dressage horse was well into her third successful year as Executive Director of the International Equestrian Association in Paris; a polar bear, in the face of stiff human competition and after an impressive training camp and pre-season, had won the nod as the first-string goalie for the Toronto Maple Leafs hockey team; Google, Facebook, and Twitter were jointly funding an international educational initiative to instruct the world's animals on the productive uses, and the documented abuses, of the Internet and its social media platforms; the Chancellor of Animal Farm USA's Cyber and Polytechnic Institute, a raccoon with a Ph.D. in biochemistry from M.I.T., was also a highly-paid consultant to Unilever in London and BASF in Ludwigshafen, Germany; and birds and animals of various species were finding their way onto the boards and senior managements of North American and European companies in the agribusiness, pet food, veterinary science, perfume aromatics, travel, executive search, education, and entertainment sectors.

Animal/human diversity initiatives had become particularly robust at the high end of American and Canadian higher education. At the elite Ivy League universities and at Stanford, M.I.T., Chicago, Michigan, Berkeley, Toronto, and McGill, human parents holding progressive views not only wanted their sons and daughters to study with, and learn from, *humans* of all ages, genders, races, sexual orientations, and the like. Many insisted that their sons and daughters study and rub shoulders with the best and brightest from the animal world, too– assuming that the matriculated creatures could handle the curriculum and would not be too disruptive in the cafeterias and dorms. As one vocal parent told a Princeton University admissions officer, "And let me be clear: I want our Jessica mixing not just with the white swans but with the black swans and the brown swans too!"

A sociologist at Columbia University in New York City had developed a new metric, the Creature Diversity Index or CDI. Featuring colorful bar graphs and dense statistical tables, the CDI showed the impressive strides Columbia had made in integrating dogs, cats, horses, sheep, birds, and pigs into the university's academic and campus life–including the first-ever endowed chair devoted to World Creature Literature, restricted to nonhuman academics–and also showed, both as a point of institutional pride and as a competitive differentiator, how Columbia's bold innovations in these areas had outpaced its Ivy League rivals.

Animals with acting talent were aggressively recruited to play roles in Hollywood movies and on network and cable television in the United States, Canada, Mexico, and Europe. The Academy of Motion Picture Arts and Sciences, bowing to the general trend, had created four new Oscar categories: Best Animal Actor, or Actress, in a Leading Role; and Best Animal Actor, or Actress, in a Supporting Role. Remakes of successful animated movies using real animals in leading and supporting roles–such as *The Lion King*, *Zootopia*, *Finding Dory*, *Paddington*, and *Winnie the Pooh*– were enjoying big commercial success with human and animal audiences alike. In Hollywood and at Pinewood Studios outside of London, former dancing bears from Russia were much in demand and could basically write their own tickets, given their rigorous prior training in taking human direction. And animal-directed American, Canadian, Mexican, British, Irish, French, and German films featuring human casts, and animal-directed documentaries (for example, on the dire effects of climate change on various nonhuman species), were no longer the once-in-a-blue-moon event they once were. (The human entertainment industry was, however, less supportive of animals playing leading human roles in big-budget Hollywood films, especially in political thrillers and serious drama. As one Hollywood studio executive blurted out, in a pitch meeting where a talent agent from William Morris was touting his Tony-Award-winning kangaroo client for the role of Hamlet in a new, big-budget movie based on Shakespeare's famous play, "Hey, Gabe–I mean, we're as progressive as the next studio, but could you give us a *break* here!")

In the decades following the Creature Insurrection, the variety of nonhuman species represented in positions of political leadership was also noteworthy. The animal nations located in France, Germany, Ireland, the United Kingdom, the United States, Canada, Russia, China, Mexico, and Tibet could boast presidents drawn from a wide variety of animal, bird, and fish species–including a current presidential crop comprising a Gallic rooster (France), an eagle (Germany), a salmon (Ireland), a lioness (United Kingdom), a raven (United States), a beaver (Canada), a black grizzly bear (Russian Federation), a black and white panda bear (China), a chihuahua (Mexico), and a black-necked crane (Tibet).

In matters of business, pigs had played commanding roles at the animal communities located in North America and Europe; had aggressively exploited and expanded business opportunities both within and beyond their respective animal nations; and were prominently represented on annual lists of the world's richest animals.

But no pig, male or female, had ever won a presidential election. Indeed, the pigs' despotic rule at the original animal community in England had become such a prominent feature in the education of young birds and other animals that no pig had ventured even to run for the presidency of any animal nation. The non-pig majorities had long memories and, evidently, the stench created by Napoleon and his cruel pig enablers still lingered.

At Animal Farm USA, however, something new and unprecedented was afoot. A prominent pig entrepreneur, television producer, media celebrity, real estate tycoon, international playboy, and tireless self-promoter had boldly splashed onto the political scene and was bestriding the news and media worlds of Animal Farm and other animal nations like a Colossus (fittingly, given that the show name under which he had been exhibited as a younger pig was Colossal Boar.)

The pigs at Animal Farm USA and elsewhere in North America and abroad, who rarely got excited about anything except food and money, were in ecstasies: for the first time since the Creature Insurrection, a pig had thrown his tail into the ring and would vie for the presidency of Animal Farm.

And not just any pig, but the biggest pig of them all.

CHAPTER 4

From the day he was born, in a private heated nursery at Animal Farm USA, Big Pig was destined to be an exceptional pig. Although many newborn piglets are confused and disoriented and need to be guided to their mothers' teats, not Big Pig. From his first waking moments, he expertly homed in on them and was also unusual in making determined efforts to suckle not at just one or two of his mother's teats but at all of them and in no particular order–even if that meant pushing and nosing aside some of his newborn siblings who were also trying to suckle for nourishment. Big Pig was even known to suckle at the teats of other nursing sows when the occasion presented itself (variety being the spice of life and, as he would often joke with his male pigster friends, "Any teat in a storm, right?")

All of the other weaners at Animal Farm, including his pig siblings, quickly outgrew the heat lamps that were used to keep them warm during their infancy. Big Pig, however, continued to use a heat lamp into adulthood. When asked to explain this unusual practice, his answer was simple and unapologetic: he liked, and was given to understand that the many ladies of his acquaintance also liked, the urbane, tanned look it bestowed on his thick pink skin (except around his eyes, which he sensibly protected by wearing tanning goggles.) And while most male pigs at the farm gave no thought to the bristles on their snout and face, Big Pig had always taken care from an early age to make sure that his bristles were expertly trimmed, sprayed, and neatly combed.

Big Pig was born with exceptionally strong legs; his mother had told him that he had practically walked out of her womb and then started running in circles around her and skipping about on his hooves as she was giving birth to his seven siblings. That Big Pig's legs were unusually thick and strong was a blessing, for they were destined to support a huge bulk: at two years' old, Big Pig weighed almost seven hundred pounds. It was this impressive bulk which, prior to the start of his adult career in the family's real estate business, had earned him the show name, Colossal Boar. And having acquired, early in his childhood, a passion for the amusements of the golf course, Big Pig's portly frame also enabled him, while standing confidently on his stout hind legs, to hit long tee shots with a custom-designed driver he held between the knuckles of his trotter.

Everyone had heard of Big Pig. By his own admission, he was the smartest and most famous pig he knew and, not coincidentally, the most skilled self-promoter. More than any other prominent pig or other animal in the United States or abroad, Big Pig had learned to exploit the power of social media to spark controversy and keep his name before the public. His iconic Twitter handle, @realBigPig, was instantly recognizable and his incessant tweets–"liked" or not–were followed, and often retweeted and commented upon, by millions.

Big Pig's father, a shrewd Large White boar who had made pioneering inroads into the worlds of both animal and human commercial and residential real estate, had given him his start in the family business and Big Pig had shown a real flair for it. When his father passed away, Big Pig changed the name of the family firm to Big Pig Enterprises, Inc.; rebranded the many buildings and golf courses he owned, and branded some new ones still under construction, with names like The Big Pig Power Tower in midtown Manhattan, Place du Big Pig in Paris, The Royal Pig Big Albion at Canary Wharf in London, and The Big Pig Swing Away Golf & Country Club in Westchester County, New York; and also branched out into the manufacture and marketing of custom-made luxury accessories that catered to wealthy pigs at Animal Farm USA and at the other animal-led communities in Canada, Mexico, the United Kingdom, Ireland, France, Germany, and Tibet, and also to the fabulously wealthy pig and bear oligarchs in Russia and China who lived like modern-day Romanovs and Medicis.

In only a few years, Big Pig Enterprises was a

force to be reckoned with in high-end commercial and residential real estate (including luxury resorts and specially-designed par-three golf courses for "creatures of means") and held a virtual monopoly in the luxury market for gold troughs, gold wallows, gold toilets, gold bidets, gold sinks, gold utensils, gold plate, gold goblets, and other gold home accessories for wealthy swine in North America and elsewhere.

In morals, Big Pig was something between a carnival barker and a used-car salesman. Veracity, empathy, self-respect, and modesty were not qualities required from him by the world. He had the vices, but none of the compensating virtues, common among men set from birth to occupy high places and long accustomed to being coddled, flattered, and obeyed in all things. As the unquestioned leader of his own sprawling business empire, he had a strong affinity for other authoritarian leaders whose word was law, whether in business or in politics. Big Pig embraced the authoritarian's worldview that, from time immemorial, governments have been filled with the most corrupt humans and animals; that high political office was fruitful of hypocrites; that high-sounding rhetoric from the ruling classes about working tirelessly "for the good of the people" was merely a smokescreen behind which they could more readily line their own pockets; and that, if the ruling classes could get away with lucrative hypocrisy and hokum of that sort, decade after decade, it was only fair that others be given a chance to slurp at the government trough too.

Big Pig shared other traits prominent among authoritarian leaders: the quality he most prized, in others, was loyalty; if you crossed him, the animosities he harbored were bitter, enduring, and public; and except when issuing insults to underlings in his presence, no one had ever seen him laugh.

Big Pig's much-publicized exploits with the fairer sex over the years (and not just with sows) were regularly featured in Animal Farm tabloids and in the gutter press in Beaverville, Albion, and some of the other European animal communities. Many of the females who dated Big Pig recounted that, although he could be charming and always took them to the most expensive restaurants and the most exclusive and discreet hotels, his sensuality was coarse and unrefined. For the animals and humans who knew Big Pig best, those reports were unsurprising. From a young age, the admiration and desire Big Pig felt for female sows and other animals were not mingled with respect or affection or with any chivalrous sentiment. Big Pig sometimes joked that one of his life's great pleasures was getting his friends' wives into bed and remarked to his male pigster friends, after a new sexual conquest and always with a snicker, "That's the thing about sucking on teats. It starts when you're a baby and you just never outgrow it!"

As was true of other prominent males of Big

Pig's acquaintance, on the frequent occasions when Big Pig's sexual attentions were unwanted or rebuffed–typically by a younger female who either worked for Big Pig or over whom Big Pig could exert leverage of some sort–his vanity could not brook the rejection and the situation got out of hand. The large number of females who had come forward with credible allegations that Big Pig had forced his unwanted attentions on them or had touched them without their consent were promptly paid off in order to keep them quiet. Notwithstanding these serial payoffs and often in the face of video, photographic, or tape-recorded evidence to the contrary, Big Pig told reporters from *The Creature Enquirer* and other tabloids that "*no one* is more respectful to women than Big Pig" and that in most cases he did not even know, or had not even met, the females in question, whom he referred to dismissively as Sow #1, Sow #2, Sow #3, Sow #4, Sow #5, and so forth. And when some of those females pressed their claims or otherwise crossed him, Big Pig resorted to calling them names such as "Horseface," "a crazed, crying lowlife," "a dog and a liar" and, in one instance, momentarily forgetting his own lineage, as having "the face of a pig."

Like his father before him, Big Pig saw golden opportunities in the Sovietski Farm commercial and residential real estate markets and had aggressively cultivated Russian bear leaders and oligarchs to get their blessing to build a new luxury high-rise in Grizliski, the capital city of Sovietski Farm, to be named The Big Pig Grand Hotel Grizliski. He openly admired, but was secretly intimidated by, Bully Bear, the wily grizzly bear who had long held the simultaneous roles of President of Sovietski Farm and patriarch of the group of Russian bears who had seized power at Sovietski Farm in the tumult that followed the breakup of the Soviet Union and had ruthlessly transformed that power into vast riches for themselves and their friends and loyal retainers.

Big Pig's wariness of Bully Bear was well-founded. Many of Bully Bear's political opponents and business adversaries were either exceptionally careless or exceptionally unlucky. Animals, and even a few humans, who had crossed Bully Bear shared the disconcerting habit of dying suddenly by strange misadventure–whether by drowning in shallow water, or being struck by lightning on a cloudless day, or falling into a tar pit or a large hole filled with poured concrete, or having all of their vital organs fail simultaneously and their blood and skin turn radioactive (and in one puzzling case, right after the unfortunate victim, the outspoken leader of a fledgling political party opposing Bully Bear's iron rule at Sovietski Farm, had got a clean bill of health from his personal physician.)

In his waning years, Big Pig's father had experienced a series of financial reversals and the financing behind Big Pig Enterprises was the source of frequent speculation in the business press. But within a year of taking over as Chairman and Chief Executive Officer of Big Pig Enterprises, Big Pig casually let it be known that, in the objective estimate of the family's longtime accountant, he was the world's richest pig.

As the world's richest pig, Big Pig reasoned that he must also be a deep thinker. In a lengthy biographical piece featuring a regal-looking Big Pig on its cover, the animal edition of *Time* magazine took serious issue with that claim and wrote that "Big Pig's deep thoughts seem never to rise to the surface or find expression in his words or deeds." Commenting on Big Pig's documented propensity for lying, *Time* cited Mark Twain and speculated that Big Pig "would rather tell seven lies than make one explanation" and that "perhaps Big Pig lies so much just to keep in practice."

But if Big Pig possessed only average intelligence and well-below-average veracity, no one doubted his high degree of low cunning, his gift for getting his own way, and his skill in getting the last laugh on the animals and humans who had underestimated him. Part of what made Big Pig's success in the business and media worlds so puzzling and even infuriating to some was the fact that, given his expensive private school and university education, Big Pig was surprisingly ill-read, ill-informed, and inarticulate. Buying and selling high-end commercial and residential real estate and purveying gold home accessories to rich pigs and foreign oligarchs did not, however, require erudition or a basic knowledge of national and world affairs or even a serviceable vocabulary. What it did require, and what Big Pig supplied in abundance, was coolness under pressure, a talent for exploiting the vanity of the ultrarich, and a gift for breathless hyperbole ("the *Lamborghini* of elite office buildings"; "not just gracious penthouse living but the *ultimate* in gracious penthouse living"; "as *deluxe* as it gets"; "a *priceless* gem"; "the *gold standard* in pig toilets and bidets"; "a *steal* at five hundred million.")

And whatever else you could say about Big Pig–and there were always lots of folks, whether animal or human, who were prepared to say plenty, in print, on television, and in the twittersphere–he had the flamboyance of a confidence man; a flair for being constantly in the news (it was often joked that the most dangerous place at Animal Farm USA was the patch of ground between Big Pig and a television camera or microphone); and an unerring eye for the distressed commercial or residential property which, with some tasteful renovation, could quickly be resold at a handsome profit.

Big Pig had long toyed with the idea of playing on an even bigger stage and running for the presidency of Animal Farm. The time was *now*, he finally told himself. He had humongous name recognition, an attractive new wife, a stable family life, a huge following on all social media platforms, and more than enough money to finance his own campaign. Perhaps most importantly, he was unaware of any female who possessed incriminating facts about him who had not already been paid to keep quiet and signed an ironclad confidentiality agreement. And Animal Farm's incumbent president, the highly educated and widely admired Sage Raven, was nearing the end of his second term and could not, under Animal Farm's constitution, run for a third one–so Big Pig would not have to face the prospect of challenging a popular incumbent.

Sage Raven's handpicked successor, Henrietta Hen, was extraordinarily well-funded and a formidable campaigner in her own right. But she was also, in Big Pig's estimation, uninspiring, overconfident, and even, perhaps, beatable. Given the vivid impression Henrietta and her large team of publicists had created that the next presidential election at Animal Farm would be more a coronation than a real contest, Big Pig guessed that other prominent citizens with presidential ambitions would be disinclined to take on Henrietta and would bide their time for a year or two until she was safely off the stage. Big Pig had also made a shrewd bet, if only to himself, that enough time had now passed since the pigs' betrayal and ouster at the original animal community in England and that the time was now ripe for a pig of international standing and accomplishments to throw his tail into the presidential ring at Animal Farm.

The idea was not to *win* the presidency, Big Pig knew. Winning might reduce his autonomy and flexibility in running Big Pig Enterprises as he

saw fit and curtail his treasured weekly golf out-
ings and other extracurricular amusements. No,
the idea was merely to run for the presidency. A
presidential run would put him constantly in the
news; enhance his personal profile and corporate
brand; make him some new and potentially valuable business connections; and maybe even im-
prove his chances of getting Bully Bear's green
light to build The Big Pig Grand Hotel Grizliski at
Sovietski Farm. And after making a respectable
and better-than-expected showing against the formidable female candidate whom everyone predicted would be the hands-down winner, he would
sit back and watch the lucrative business, public
speaking, and television offers flood in.

Big Pig had come to a decision and began to
take steps to enlist his family in the effort. He was
confident that they would embrace the strategy
and come along for the ride. His presidential run
was, after all, only a glorified vanity play and his
wife and adult children, some of whom had started
their own businesses by trading shamelessly on
the "Big Pig" name and brand, knew all about
vanity plays.

Big Pig's fourth wife, Voluptua, was a sleek
leopardess and former advertising agency executive who valued her privacy, was a hard-headed
realist about her husband's infidelities, and was
more than a little ambivalent about his decision
to run for the presidency. But Big Pig assured
her that he would not, and almost certainly could

not, prevail in a presidential contest against the heavily-favored and prodigiously-funded Henrietta Hen and Voluptua, though not sophisticated in the ways of politics, had come to the same conclusion. Big Pig's adult children showed no such ambivalence: they were "all in" and looked forward to the reflected glory in which their father's presidential run would permit them to bask.

At a private dinner the day after he had got the green light from Voluptua, one of Big Pig's many high-level media contacts–a veteran CEO whose news organization had covered leadership contests for many years, at Animal Farm, Beaverville, and other animal-led nations–advised Big Pig and Voluptua that, in terms of sheer return on investment, the lucrative opportunities that would follow even an unsuccessful presidential run were well worth the time, effort, and money expended. The whole idea, Big Pig explained to Voluptua on their way home from the dinner, was to build up his national and international brand and name recognition and, after the election, exploit the new business opportunities in television and commercial real estate, not to mention the six-figure public-speaking fees, that would roll his way.

When Voluptua fretted to her longtime assistant, Charmayne, about the heightened media scrutiny they would all be subjected to during a hard-fought presidential campaign, Charmayne did her best to console her: "Miss Voluptua, I've never been through one of these either, obviously, but it will probably just suck for a while and then it will be over and we'll all get back to life in the penthouse suite–when your toughest decision will be whether your new party gown will be a Valentino or a Vera Wang."

Having decided to take the presidential plunge, Big Pig started looking around for a campaign manager. Although there were many things, even many important things, which Big Pig didn't know that he didn't know, Big Pig did know that, having never before run for political office, he needed a campaign manager. He made a number of discreet inquiries among his wealthy friends and business associates and the name that kept coming up was that of a human, Silas Cain. In a long and distinguished career in political consulting, Silas Cain had helped Crafty Coyote, Sage Raven's predecessor, win two successive presidential elections and had also had his fair share of wins in human gubernatorial elections in Texas, Arizona, and California, and for U.S. Senate seats in New York, Maryland, Virginia, and Florida.

When Big Pig reached out to him, Cain was intrigued. He had heard from his own sources that the business community at Animal Farm was desperately looking for a business-friendly candidate to take on what one CEO described as the "Henrietta Hen juggernaut." Cain agreed to travel from Washington, D.C., to Animal Farm the next day and meet with Big Pig and, separately, with Voluptua. Cain knew Big Pig only by reputation but had reached the same conclusion as Big Pig: that a well-financed, straight-talking, disruptive political outsider might have at least a puncher's chance against Henrietta Hen and her well-oiled political machine.

Cain arrived at Big Pig's sprawling ranch a little after lunch the next day. Voluptua greeted him at the door and explained that she only needed a few minutes with him and could he please look her up on his way out. Cain agreed and was escorted into Big Pig's spacious, heat-lamped study. Cain was impressed by the ease, even the studied grace, with which Big Pig walked gingerly but confidently on his two hind legs and then settled his seven-hundred-pound bulk onto the long leather sofa and motioned Cain to do the same.

Having heard several reports about Big Pig's nonexistent reading habits and that Big Pig, on matters of history, government, and government policy, had the knowledge and opinions of a child, Cain was tempted to check whether any of the hundreds of expensive, leather-bound books tightly arrayed on the floor-to-ceiling oak bookshelves had ever been cracked open. And having also read that dogs–even languid, friendly dogs never known to have barked before–unaccountably became vicious in Big Pig's presence and snarled and barked at him as he passed, Cain made a mental note that if he were engaged by Big Pig he would depute the candidate's eldest daughter, Pigletta, to work the dog vote.

After exchanging the customary pleasantries, they launched into a wide-ranging conversation about the state of the Animal Farm nation; about Big Pig's vision for "Putting Animal Farm First"; and about the ways in which Cain could help Big Pig create and execute a strategy that might give him a reasonable shot at winning the presidency.

Big Pig had dictated to his secretary a list of his key differences with Sage Raven's ambitious regulatory and internationalist agenda and tried to articulate them to Cain. But Big Pig's presentation was rambling, disorganized, and at several points barely intelligible. By the time Big Pig had finished, Cain had distilled the two or three talking points worth mentioning: the dramatic increase in the regulation of Animal Farm businesses–everything from more stringent wage and hour laws, to enhanced worker protections against species and gender discrimination, to tighter emission-control standards at Animal Farm's factories and oil refineries–all of which increased compliance costs for Animal Farm's businesses and rendered them less profitable and internationally competitive; unacceptably weak border control along the entire length of Animal Farm's thirty-mile southern border with Casa Chihuahua, the Mexican animal-led community, coupled with liberal asylum and visa policies that permitted, even encouraged, foreign animals born and raised in Mexico and in Central and South America to gain entry (using Casa Chihuahua as an entry point), achieve eventual citizenship, and take jobs away from hardworking natural-born citizens; and, more generally, Sage Raven's (and, if elected, Henrietta Hen's) radically outward-looking stance that valued multiculturalism and international alliances over the sovereignty and independence of the world's richest and most powerful animal nation.

Cain explained to Big Pig that his natural constituency was not college-educated and reasonably well-to-do animals who subscribed to *The New York Review of Books* or watched *Frontline* on PBS, but rather the *very* wealthy, who clamored for lower individual, estate, and corporate tax rates and less government regulation, on the one hand, and native born, law-abiding, non-college-educated animals of all species who were struggling just to pay their bills, send their offspring to college, and maintain their shaky status in the middle or lower-middle class, on the other. Cain told Big Pig that it might be possible to craft a winning coalition comprising those two broad groups and that there was probably a large number of animal voters of all species, male *and* female and in every socioeconomic group, who were not quite ready to elect a female president–but who were also not quite ready to admit that they were not quite ready. He also suggested that Big Pig possessed a rare gift which, if properly exploited, might make all the difference in an insurgent, underdog campaign: the ability to enrage and dishearten his political adversaries while, at the same time, motivating and energizing his core electoral base.

Cain advised Big Pig to present himself as a selfless, patriotic, unapologetically wealthy citizen whose sound business instincts and growth-oriented strategies would help other animals climb the economic ladder too. If Big Pig could appeal to high net-worth animals and the ultrarich–and also to the embattled middle class and to the militant flag-wavers and closet misogynists–he could make the presidential race interesting and maybe even pull off a stunning upset.

Big Pig pleaded a natural necessity and, while he was out of the room, Cain chuckled to himself about how, in his pitch to Big Pig, he had almost convinced himself that Big Pig could make the presidential race interesting. Privately, Cain had strong misgivings. Henrietta Hen actually knew something about government and international relations, was an effective and tireless campaigner, and was backed by Sage Raven and virtually the entire Animal Farm political establishment. And though she was not a compelling public speaker, Henrietta had at least fifty I.Q. points on Big Pig and, sooner rather than later, that stark discrepancy in intelligence and mental agility would show. Cain shuddered to think what Henrietta could do to Big Pig in a live, ninety-minute television debate: it would be like watching Tom Brady and the New England Patriots take on the local high school football team. (Mixing his sports metaphors, Cain also thought that if he accepted this engagement he would need to bring a white towel to the debate studio so that he could "throw in the towel" if Henrietta was landing too many eye-scratching left jabs and head-snapping karate kicks, and had Big Pig on the ropes.)

Still, Cain mused, he would be well-paid for his efforts; he would gain major brownie points with the wealthy human financiers and industrialists in whose circles he moved (after all, no other animal had stepped up to take on Henrietta Hen and it was undignified to lose a presidential election by default); and preventing the pig from being trounced by the hen would vindicate Cain's deeply-held conviction that presidential elections should be robust contests between contrasting political and geopolitical visions and not mere coronations for retreaded politicians like Henrietta Hen–who seemed to think that, if only she hung around long enough, everyone would simply agree that it was her turn to govern.

Cain knew that he could help Big Pig make his case to the citizens of Animal Farm and also knew that anything less than an embarrassingly lopsided electoral defeat would be accounted a moral victory. Besides, it would all be over in a month or so and whatever else you could say about Big Pig, you couldn't say he wasn't entertaining.

It occurred to Cain that Big Pig was like the statue in the Greek myth, Pygmalion–and that perhaps, in a subtle twist on the Pygmalion story, it was Cain's destiny to breathe political life into that statue and cause others to fall in love with it, even if he himself couldn't. Win or lose, Cain thought, he might even rate a mention in the history books for modernizing a Greek myth: Pigmalion.

Cain had decided. He was *in*, if Big Pig wanted him.

When Big Pig returned to the study, Cain told him that he thought he could help Big Pig run a strong campaign about which they could both be proud.

Big Pig was elated and asked Cain to call him in the morning so that they could finalize the fee arrangements and start thinking about a campaign announcement.

Cain looked for Voluptua on his way out and found her waiting for him in the high-ceilinged entrance foyer.

"Hi, Voluptua. I understand you wanted a quick word?"

"Yes, Silas. Thank you. I have just one question. *He can't possibly win, right?*"

Cain smiled and answered matter-of-factly: "Not a snowball's chance in hell."

Voluptua, visibly relieved, placed her perfumed left paw gently on Cain's right foot and looked up at him gratefully. "God bless you for saying that!"

At the beginning, when the laws of Animal Farm USA were first formulated, the group of distinguished animal and bird elders from Texas, California, and New York who had agreed to assist in putting some basic constitutional structures in place made a number of sensible approximations to the government structures of the United States of America. But since the original animal farm in England had no written constitution, the elders had no formal model of animal governance to imitate and concluded that the blueprint for their new animal-led community needed to acknowledge the vast differences in history and culture, and in social and financial complexity, between a fledgling animal nation, on the one hand, and the mature human liberal democracy and world economic powerhouse that had sponsored it, on the other.

The elders also believed that, at least in the early years of Animal Farm USA's existence, when so much needed to be accomplished so quickly, an elected president with broad executive powers was called for. In that spirit, Animal Farm's framers drafted a written constitution that was brief, vaguely worded, and granted expansive powers to the chief executive. The constitution provided that there would be a president of Animal Farm, to be elected annually and for a maximum of two, one-year terms. The president would act as Animal Farm's chief executive and would have authority, by Executive Order, to make annual expenditures up to an amount approved by a majority of popular votes cast at the time of each presidential election. The president was also authorized to take such other steps, by Executive Order, as he or she thought appropriate for the protection and well-being of Animal Farm and its citizens.

Election campaigns were limited to three weeks and, if more than one citizen announced his or her candidacy for president, there would be at least one presidential debate.

The constitution provided for no legislative branch or Bill of Rights and Animal Farm USA's judicial branch comprised a small number of village-like courts superintended by private animal citizens appointed by the president. The courts would adjudicate, on a part-time basis, legal matters brought to their attention by animal citizens living in a given Animal Farm sector. The matters routinely heard by the judges all sprang from a simple but comprehensive provision modeled on the French Civil Code, which provided that "any act of animal or man, which causes damages to another animal, shall oblige the animal or man by whose fault it occurred to repair it."

The constitution could be amended by a

plebiscite vote, but only if two stringent require-
ments were met: the amendment needed to be
approved by the individual votes of at least two
thirds of all eligible voters and also needed to be
approved by the majority vote of at least two thirds
of each animal species living at Animal Farm.

Having created a government in which the
president enjoyed broad powers, the framers were
under no illusions that, for the whole system to
work, the elected president needed to be honest,
capable, and elected by a relatively broad spec-
trum of Animal Farm's different animal species.
The framers hoped that the "electoral college" set
forth in the constitution would help ensure that
result.

Animal Farm USA's electoral college was modeled on the United States Constitution. The units
of the electoral college were not States (since
Animal Farm had a unitary government and had
no "States") but rather the different animal, bird,
insect, and fish species that inhabited Animal Farm
at any given time. Depending on its population
in the most recent triennial census, each animal
species was allotted a specific number of "electoral
votes" and, for simplicity's sake, the constitution
set the total number of electoral votes at one
hundred.

A candidate for president needed to win at least
fifty-one electoral votes to win the presidency or,
where there were more than two presidential candidates, had to win more electoral votes than any

other candidate, provided that he or she won at least thirty-four electoral votes. Eligibility to vote was determined by each animal species. The criterion used by most species was "the rule of quarters," namely, if you had attained an age that was at least one-quarter of the average life expectancy of your species and your birthday was at least sixty days before the presidential election, you were eligible to vote.

Electoral votes were awarded on the basis of the popular votes of each animal species. For example, if crows were allotted three electoral votes, then all three electoral votes would be awarded to the presidential candidate who captured the largest number of votes cast by crows. Special provision was made for Animal Farm's insect species, given the logistical difficulties associated with having millions of ants, spiders, bees, and other insects vote every year. Somewhat arbitrarily, the Animal Farm constitution awarded the insects, in the aggregate, five electoral votes out of the total of one hundred. The insects were required to appoint, at least two weeks before election day, a single insect to cast their five electoral votes and typically chose the most prominent Queen Bee to discharge that important civic duty.

In the dozens of prior presidential elections at Animal Farm USA, voter suppression and voter fraud had never been a serious issue and in many of those elections a single consensus candidate had emerged and the outcome was a mere formality (the uncontested election from a year before, resulting in a second presidential term for Sage Raven, being the most recent example).

But with Sage Raven's tenure as President entering its final month–and with rumors widely circulating that the imminent election might pit two well-known, aggressively ambitious, and deep-pocketed citizens against each other–many pundits speculated that this time might be different.

At 3 p.m. on the last day for filing the papers necessary to be listed on the presidential ballot and with the election to succeed Sage Raven only twenty-two days away, no citizen had yet declared his or her candidacy and the rumor mills were working overtime. Big Pig broke the suspense by filing his registration papers just after three o'clock. He immediately issued a tweet announcing that his inaugural speech as a presidential candidate would be delivered the following day and that it would be "must-sea TV" (which, after an awkward exchange with one of Silas Cain's young staffers, Big Pig reissued as "must-see TV.")

Henrietta Hen's candidacy papers were signed, dated, and ready to go, but she had purposely waited to file them. Henrietta calculated that Big Pig, being the seven-hundred-pound marshmallow she thought he really was, might wimp out at the last minute and that she could file her papers just before the 5 p.m. deadline and coast to victory in an uncontested "coronation" like the one Sage Raven had enjoyed twelve months before. With that hope having been dashed by Big Pig's announcement, Henrietta filed her candidacy papers and the game was afoot.

The citizens of Animal Farm knew that they were about to witness an election campaign unprecedented in the nation's history and that, in three weeks' time, Animal Farm would have either its first female, or its first pig, president.

Henrietta Hen had enjoyed a long and distinguished career in the upper crust of Animal Farm's business and government establishments. After breaking through one glass ceiling after another to become the first female CEO of Haute Couture Femelle, an international fashion house specializing in pant suits and other business attire for female humans, chickens, geese, turkeys, ducks, and other fowl, Henrietta's many influential friends and supporters encouraged her to enter national politics, become the first female president of Animal Farm, and shatter what had often been called "the thickest glass ceiling in the animal kingdom."

In a hard-fought and occasionally bitter presidential campaign two years before, Henrietta had been defeated by Sage Raven–notable himself for being the first all-black president of Animal Farm. With an eye to keeping her future presidential options open, Henrietta had agreed to become Sage Raven's principal advisor on domestic and international affairs and had helped him to execute important initiatives shoring up Animal Farm's flagging economy and recommitting the nation to longstanding international agreements with the animal communities in Canada, Mexico, the United Kingdom, France, and Germany whose purpose was to check the aggressive expansionist policies of Sovietski Farm and the Animal People's Republic of China.

As a key player in Sage Raven's administration, Henrietta had gained international praise and notoriety for calling out Bully Bear, Sovietski Farm's leader, as a murderous authoritarian who tolerated no dissent and whom the animal world would be well rid of. In the face of Bully Bear's public threats of retaliation, Henrietta succeeded in persuading Sage Raven and the leaders of other animal nations to impose a series of stiff economic sanctions on Sovietski Farm that had infuriated Bully Bear and had rendered Sovietski Farm's faltering economy even more fragile than it was already.

Henrietta's domestic and diplomatic successes and her talent for grabbing headlines without appearing to be too brazen about it had made her a household name. As one neutral observer wrote in his weekly internet blog, "Henrietta Hen is perhaps the only animal in the United States, other than Sage Raven, whose name recognition rivals Big Pig's." Her recent autobiography, *Henrietta: A Hen's Life*, had become an international bestseller in seventeen animal languages (including audio-only versions in the sophisticated polytonal languages of Duck, Whale, and Dolphin, narrated with considerable vocal skill by Henrietta herself) and had also sold well with human readers.

During her two-year stint as Sage Raven's principal advisor, Henrietta had been coy about whether she still harbored presidential ambitions. But as one editorial writer observed, the only known cure for the presidential itch was embalming fluid. The conventional wisdom among the political classes held that Henrietta would unquestionably run to succeed Sage Raven; that she would enjoy Sage Raven's rock-solid support; that her election as Animal Farm's first female president was a virtual lock; and that other animals with presidential ambitions were best advised to sit it out until after Henrietta had had her turn.

Henrietta's development of policy positions for her presidential campaign was rigorous, evidence-based, and comprehensive. She had briefing books, five-point plans, and seven-point proposals on every conceivable issue: the benefits of prudent regulation; the downsides to imprudent over-regulation; the soon-to-be-irreversible effects of climate change; the leverage the animals and birds needed to exert on human governments to get the humans to address climate change; the importance of Animal Farm's geostrategic alliances; the threats posed by Bully Bear's authoritarian regime at Sovietski Farm; the proper balance between border security and the issuance of visas to asylum seekers, skilled workers, and other animals who sought admission to Animal Farm; the benefits of international free-trade agreements for the average citizen, and a host of others.

The briefing books, five-point plans, and seven-point proposals were not just for show. Henrietta Hen knew what was in them and could provide informed and thoughtful answers to just about any question that could arise on the campaign trail. Her superb mastery of the issues did, however, come at a cost: she regularly put her campaign crowds, television viewers, and assorted other supporters to sleep in the course of demonstrating that mastery.

Big Pig, by contrast, had no mastery of the issues; had no interest in achieving mastery of the issues; had no conception of what it might be like to possess knowledge or insights even remotely approaching mastery of the issues; and seemed to lack the intellectual curiosity or capacity to understand anything more complex than the sorts of insults that would really get under Henrietta Hen's skin or simple facts like, because fifty-one was one more than half of one hundred, he needed fifty-one electoral votes to win the election.

Early on, Silas Cain had concluded that it was futile to give Big Pig too much to think about at any one time and resolved to adapt his campaign teaching methods to what he facetiously called "Big Pig's unique learning style." Cain had heard from Big Pig's longtime personal accountant and had deduced for himself after his introductory meeting with the candidate at Animal Farm that Big Pig was a "one-minute man"—namely, that Big Pig's limited attention span could only handle memos or talking points presented on a single sheet of paper and, preferably, on the top half of a single sheet of paper.

In the days following his engagement as Big Pig's campaign manager, Cain had joked with his staff that in any one-page memo to the candidate, the really critical stuff needed to be placed "above the fold." Reacting to Cain's comment, one of his young staffers suggested, tongue in cheek, that maybe the campaign memos to Big Pig should just be a series of emojis, question marks, and exclamation points. Much to the young staffer's surprise, Cain told her that the idea had real merit and instructed her to start working on it.

As it turned out, the memos and talking points prepared for Big Pig's television appearances and other campaign events were heavily inspired by comic book treatments of action heroes like Superman, Batman, and Captain America–where the villains were powerful, dark, and dastardly and where the heroic exploits of the larger-than-life good guys were punctuated by dynamic, italicized, all-caps exclamations like *BIFF!*; *BANG!*; *BONK!*; *ZAP!*; and *ZOWIE!*

And given the segment of the electorate at which his appeals for support were targeted, Big Pig's tenth-grade vocabulary and propensity to communicate only in shopworn clichés were a big advantage when it came to speechmaking. Silas Cain had assured Big Pig that if the message and the messenger were right, average law-abiding Animal Farm citizens struggling to maintain their living standards in a fast-changing global economy could be whipped up into a frenzy of political passion, activism, and xenophobia which, with a break or two, might actually get him elected. What was needed, Cain urged, were "red meat" speeches that played viscerally to the animals' sense of class and species solidarity, unmerited economic victimization, and disdain for other animals or other animal species not native to Animal Farm. Cain was confident that Big Pig's speeches, if delivered with just the right mix of conviction and resentment, would elicit noisy, primal chants of support for Big Pig that might attract other disgruntled animal voters watching on TV.

Big Pig channeled Cain's advice and promised to treat each election crowd and television interviewer to pithy, take-no-prisoners rants combining xenophobia, virulent resentment, fake populism, and locker-room vulgarity.

Big Pig's speech announcing his presidential candidacy featured the dark conspiratorial themes that would recur in all of his later speeches, punctuated by hard-edged slogans that his campaign operatives were paid to start chanting at key points in the speech (the well-paid operatives also carried hand-painted "Big Pig for President!" and "Pen the Hen!" banners that looked, and were intended to look, homemade, but were actually produced and distributed by Big Pig's advance team):

"Citizens, we have the worst immigration laws in the world. You can thank Sage Raven and

Henrietta Hen for that. And what have we lost? Let me tell you what we have lost: our national identity, our international standing, our ability to control our own borders, and our commitment to putting the interests of our citizens above the interests of animals from other countries. Animal Farm has become the dumping ground for all of the other animal nations' problems and rejects. That has to stop.

"My immigration policy is simple. Here it is: 'I am sorry, *you can't come in.* Go home and take your mongrel offspring with you.' And if you want radical chihuahua terrorists, foreign-born rapists, and other lowlifes to take your jobs, molest your women folk, and make it harder for your children to achieve the same standard of living that you have worked so hard to achieve, by all means vote for Crooked Henrietta–she'll make that happen!"

At this point, a few impassioned crowd members began chanting, "PEN THE HEN!" "PEN THE HEN!" "PEN THE HEN!" and the rising chorus of "PEN THE HEN!" required Big Pig to pause until the spontaneous tribal chant died down a bit.

"You got it," Big Pig interjected. *"Pen the Hen!"*

"The hen won't keep them out," Big Pig continued. "She wants more of them to *come in*–so that they'll stay, take your jobs, become citizens, and then vote for her and her liberal friends! I will *build a wall* on our southern border, a *massive* wall, to keep them out–and I'll get the Mexican chihuahuas to pay for it!"

Spontaneous Crowd Chant: "BUILD THE WALL!" "BUILD THE WALL!" "BUILD THE WALL!"

"And you are right to believe that we live in a dangerous world and that there are animal nations out there–we all know who they are–that sometimes act against our vital national interests. Let me be clear: *nobody* will be tougher on Sovietski Farm, and on Bully Bear, than Big Pig!

"If you honor me with your vote, I intend to play big and bold on the national and international stage." (Here, the campaign script required Big Pig to look down playfully at his exposed, dangling penis.)

"Don't let *little* Crooked Henrietta, or *little* Sage Raven, or the liberal fake news media, fool you: *Size Matters!"*

Spontaneous Crowd Chant: "SIZE MATTERS!" "SIZE MATTERS!" "SIZE MATTERS!"

"Don't pay any attention to the lies Crooked Henrietta tells about me. I just laugh when she does that. I call it Henrietta's Vendetta!

"And what's with all those *pant suits*, right? I mean, doesn't she own a dress?

"Fellow citizens of Animal Farm, I am rich. I don't need, and I won't take, anyone else's money to fund my campaign. Go ask Henrietta Hen if she can make you the same promise. The hen is funded by the rich bankers and industrialists who, if she becomes president, she promises to rein in 'for the benefit of the little guy.' Does she think were we all born *last night?* Does she really think we're *that stupid?"*

Spontaneous Crowd Chant: "PEN THE HEN!" "PEN THE HEN!" "PEN THE HEN!"

"Citizens, I told you I am rich. That is just a fact. But it's an *important* fact. I am rich because I am a skilled dealmaker. The deals I make as President, on behalf of you and your hard-working families, will always put *you* first–not some immigrant thief or rapist from some shithole country where the animals don't look like us. I'll be the greatest jobs president in the history of Animal Farm. Won't that be a nice change, right?"

Spontaneous Crowd Chant: "BUILD THE WALL!" "BUILD THE WALL!" "BUILD THE WALL!"

Big Pig shook his large snout aggressively as his eyes darted around the crowd. "And if anyone gets in our way, I am going to give them some *snout*–as only *I* can do!"

"Let me make you another solemn promise. In negotiations with Animal Farm's friends and foes alike, whether animal or human, I will be *strong and steadfast*, not like the weak and mealy-mouthed Sage Raven and Crooked Henrietta." (Here, the campaign script again required that Big Pig look down at his dangling penis.)

"As each of the women in my current and past life will tell you, including my lovely wife, Voluptua, there she is in the front row–Voluptua, please stand up and be recognized–I always finish the job and *I never pull out even if the rhythm isn't right!*" (As Big Pig had predicted to Silas Cain, this line got a big response, mostly from the adult males in the audience, especially the roosters, foxes, and coyotes.)

"Citizens, I have told you what you have lost, what we have *all* lost. But truth be told, it's not what we have lost that is so infuriating. It's what's been *taken from us!*

"You want to know why I am running for President? *That* is why I am running for President.

"Only *I* can get you back what's been *taken* from you, *what's been taken from all of us!*"

Spontaneous Crowd Chant: "TAKE IT BACK!" "TAKE IT BACK!" "TAKE IT BACK!"

"When I am President, you are all going to start *winning* again.

"One last thing. As you all know, one of my core beliefs–one of the core convictions that inspired me to run for president–is my belief that, as fellow citizens of Animal Farm, we are all in this together. So my first official act as president will be to change the name of the presidential mansion from The Brick House, which does not convey the dignity, or the storied history, of that wonderful structure, to *Animal House*–which, I think you will agree, says it all!"

Spontaneous Crowd Chant: "ANIMAL HOUSE!" "ANIMAL HOUSE!" "ANIMAL HOUSE!"

"Citizens, I *want* your vote. I *need* your vote. *Together, let's take Animal Farm back again!*"

Spontaneous Crowd Chant: "TAKE IT BACK!" "TAKE IT BACK!" "TAKE IT BACK!"

"We are the United State of Animals, the most

powerful animal nation on earth. We need to *think* big! We need to *act* big! We need *Big Pig!*

"God bless all of you and God bless Animal Farm, the United State of Animals!"

Spontaneous Crowd Chant: *"THINK* BIG! *ACT* BIG! *ELECT BIG PIG!" "THINK* BIG! *ACT* BIG! *ELECT BIG PIG!" "THINK* BIG! *ACT* BIG! *ELECT BIG PIG!"*

After delivering his speech, Big Pig thanked Silas Cain for his skill in whittling down the campaign's core message to a few phrases occupying less than two lines of text on a single piece of paper and above the fold:

Pen the Hen! Build the Wall! Size Matters! Take It Back! Animal House! Think Big! Act Big! Elect Big Pig!

Big Pig was elated with the crowd's reaction to his speech and told the various well-wishers and reporters who approached him afterwards, "No one will ever forget that speech. No one. Ever."

When Silas Cain informed Big Pig that the twittersphere was "lighting up" and that the speech and national and international reactions to it were trending big-time on all social media channels, Big Pig told Cain, in an even graver tone, *"No one* will ever forget that speech. *No one. Ever."*

The reaction by Crafty Coyote, the former President of Animal Farm who had preceded Sage Raven in that role and was watching the speech split-screen, while also catching the NCAA Division I football highlights on *SportsCenter,* was less effusive but equally pithy: "That was some *weird* shit!"

At Henrietta Hen's campaign headquarters, the candidate had the same general reaction but before she could catch her breath and utter a comment, her campaign manager turned to her and exclaimed, "That was some *weird* shit!"

Sage Raven, after viewing Big Pig's speech from his presidential office at The Brick House, shook his distinguished raven head in disgusted disbelief and turned off the television.

Bully Bear, who had watched Big Pig's speech from the top floor of his elegant dacha on five thousand acres in the northeast region of Sovietski Farm, scratched his massive head with his right paw and remarked casually to his Minister of Measures and Countermeasures, the red rooster Molotov Cocktail: "That was some *weird* shit. Your job, Molotov, is to make sure that shit 'hits the fan.' The hen hates us—and the feelings are mutual. A chick victory would be very bad for us. We want the pig. When Big Pig speaks his mind, or what passes for his mind, we'll just amplify. He'll do our divisive work for us, just by tweeting and shooting off his mouth. We can weaponize his stupidity. And as you know, we have ways of putting our paws on him. I trust you know what to do."

"Yes, Leader," Molotov replied. "We have already started coordinating our efforts."

"Good. With any luck, Big Pig's arrogance and stupidity will cause real havoc not only at Animal Farm but also at the other animal communities.

That will present opportunities for us. So I'll want regular reports. And, of course, we need full deniability."

"Understood, Leader," Molotov answered, and then turned to leave.

Bully Bear wasn't done. "By the way, I trust you saw the result of yesterday's final in the World Animal Hockey Championship?"

Molotov's stomach felt queasy and he was suddenly overcome by a strong urge to urinate, right there in Bully Bear's elegantly-appointed private study. But he knew this was no time to ask for a bathroom break. "I did, Leader. Our bears played with grit and courage."

"What was the final score, Molotov?"

Molotov skipped nervously from one foot to another. "The officiating was obviously rigged. That was clear to anyone who had eyes to see!"

Bully Bear raised his voice in anger. "*What was the final score?*"

Molotov shrugged. "Five to one in favor of the Canadians."

Bully Bear leaned forward aggressively. "Molotov, this is not the first time we have had this conversation. I am getting sick and tired of the Canadian beavers defeating our Russian bears in hockey, year after year–and *really* sick of having my nose rubbed in that. After the game yesterday, Bright Beaver was interviewed and had the gall to say, 'We debate a lot of things here at Beaverville, and that's healthy. But there is always one thing that's not debatable, year in and year out: *Beaverville will win the World Animal Hockey Championship!'* He might as well have stared into the TV camera and said, 'Hey Bully Bear, this up-raised middle finger is for *you!'* This beaver is getting too cocky for his own good. What do you plan to do about that?"

"Bully Bear," Molotov pleaded, "the Canadian beavers are faster and more agile. The game is in their DNA. They literally skate circles around us. They have also developed impressive skills in pass-ing the puck between our bears' legs and slapping the puck at over one hundred miles an hour with their tails. And please remember, Canadian bea-vers invented animal hockey. At Sovietski Farm, we are making steady progress–if you recall, last year we finished third, not second. But we still have a steep hill to climb."

Bully Bear was in no mood for excuses. "Molotov, if our bear comrades can't get the job done, can we entice some Canadian beavers to take our cit-izenship and play for *us*? We'll make it worth their while. I mean, hell, we've got just as many trees, and many more and bigger lakes and rivers, than Beaverville does. And if they come over and prom-ise to help us win a hockey championship, we'll let the little buggers chew down our trees and dam up our lakes and rivers to their hearts' content!"

Molotov's bladder was fairly bursting. "Leader, I do have some further thoughts–but may I please use the bathroom? I *really* have to go."

"You can go when you and I have reached an understanding on this. You were saying?"

"Leader, we have already tried those sorts of inducements. But Bright Beaver has taken steps to foil our strategy. Beaverville is generally liberal in its trade policies, but not when it comes to hockey. Players on their national hockey team are treated like kings and queens and Bright Beaver has made it hard for them to emigrate. The game is their State religion and they've made hockey supremacy a point of national pride. And as you know, we don't make it easy for our swan ballet dancers, or our wolf or Siberian tiger violinists or pianists, to emigrate either."

Molotov, in visible discomfort now, was straining every muscle to keep from urinating on Bully Bear's paper-strewn mahogany desk.

But Bully Bear pressed on. "I don't care if the Canadian beavers invented animal hockey. *We* didn't invent deadly radioactive nerve agents or sophisticated cyber intrusions that subvert the elections of governments unfriendly to us. But through our comrades' tireless efforts, Sovietski Farm's nerve agents and cyberattacks are, by any standard, best in class. We need to add hockey to that list."

"Understood, Leader."

"I will not tolerate any more losses on the world stage in a game that our comrades have so taken to heart. By the end of next week, I want a coordinated strategy. And I don't want to hear about a 'five-year plan' or even a 'two-year plan.' I want a *six-month* plan so that this time next year I can show my own middle digit to Bright Beaver. I trust I have made myself clear?"

"Yes, Leader. Very clear."

"Good. Then make it so."

Bully Bear stared intently at Molotov for a few seconds and then stood up. "You are now excused."

CHAPTER **6**

In the first two weeks of the presidential election campaign, Big Pig's speeches drew large crowds, were covered extensively in the print and electronic media, and generated real buzz with the segment of animal voters at which they were shrewdly pitched. Big Pig always checked and was delighted to learn that his televised speeches and interviews got "great ratings" which, on a few occasions, even surpassed *The Little Pig Bachelorette* (a popular reality TV show of which Big Pig was the executive producer) and *The Creature Simpsons*.

But with the election only a week away and with Henrietta Hen still holding a substantial lead in the polls, Silas Cain determined that if Big Pig were to have any hope of eking out enough votes to make the contest close, he needed to appeal to a broader electoral base. With the poultry vote swinging heavily Henrietta's way and almost certainly a lost cause, Cain toyed with the idea of trying to clinch the equally important fox and coyote votes by dropping the mischievous line, "a chicken in every pot," into Big Pig's speeches. That line would resonate strongly with the always-ravenous foxes and coyotes who, Cain guessed, were already unenthusiastic about the prospect of a female president, especially a female *chicken* president, and wouldn't need much encouragement to get behind Big Pig.

Big Pig vetoed Cain's idea, explaining that he had dozens of influential rooster friends and business associates, and many fox and coyote friends and business associates, in the United States, Canada, and Europe and that he had some promising leads on how to get the rooster, fox, and coyote votes into his column–and maybe even some of the hens' votes too. Cain was intrigued but Big Pig was unusually closed-mouthed and circumspect and Cain decided to let the subject drop for the moment. The presidential debate was only a few days away and Cain knew that, unless Big Pig held his own against Henrietta Hen in that debate, the presidential race might be all over but the clucking.

Henrietta Hen's campaign unfolded with the ruthless efficiency Silas Cain had predicted. Like the energetic pink bunny rabbit in television commercials for batteries, Henrietta and her diverse contingent of advisors, volunteers, and canvassers "just kept on goin' and goin.'" Henrietta had raised tens of millions of dollars from donors large and small, had marshaled an impressive team of publicists and seasoned political operatives, and had secured the vocal support of virtually the entire political establishment, including Sage Raven's inner circle. Bird and animal volunteers of all ages were enthusiastically spreading her core message,

Fast Forward with Henrietta!, to the barns, pens, pastures, nests, anthills, beehives, stores, office buildings, factories, oil rigs, and oil refineries in every sector of Animal Farm.

Confronted daily by Big Pig's louche insults ("Crooked Henrietta!"; "Pen the Hen!") and misogyny, Henrietta had made a strategic decision to keep to the high road and let voters contrast her smooth civility and broad government experience with Big Pig's oafish vulgarity and cluelessness on policy. In that spirit, she had vetoed the proposed campaign slogans, "If it walks like a pig and talks like a pig …"; "Big Pig: A Pig in Sheep's Clothing"; and (her favorite) "Calling All Millionaires: Pig Out with Big Pig!"

Her deliberately low-key campaign strategy was working: every reputable public opinion poll had her well ahead, both in the popular vote and in the electoral college. And she was confident that her policy mastery, meticulously-prepared briefing books, and well-honed debating skills would serve her well in the upcoming presidential debate and that a decisive debate win might hammer the final nail in Big Pig's political coffin.

Debate preparations in Big Pig's camp were of an entirely different character. There were no briefing books, because Big Pig didn't read. There were no mock debates, because Big Pig got upset if you asked him a question, not that he couldn't answer, but that he couldn't remember the pre-prepared, canned answer to. Forced to improvise, Cain directed one of his staffers to record possible debate questions and short, carefully-crafted answers on an iPhone–so that Big Pig would be spared the burden of reading and would only have to listen to the recording and memorize a few key phrases. But that didn't work, either, because Big Pig protested that listening to the recording would disrupt his upcoming golf dates and cut into his Faux News and *Little Pig Bachelorette* TV time. And when an exasperated Cain asked Big Pig if it would be possible to make arrangements to play the recording at low volume while Big Pig was sleeping, Big Pig objected, reasonably enough, that there were other things he preferred to do when he was in bed at night with Voluptua.

With plans A, B, and C having been rejected outright and with the televised presidential debate only two days away, Cain pivoted decisively to Plan D: the single piece of paper. Cain and his staff prepared a one-page memo to Big Pig featuring, as its sole content, two illustrations and accompanying captions: on the top half of the page, titled "My Domestic Policy," a cartoon picture of a shrieking hen in a powder-blue pants suit, head cocked severely to one side and bill wide open, under which was written, in all caps, "CROOKED HENRIETTA!" "THAT *CLUCKING* HENRIETTA!" "PEN THE HEN!"; and on the bottom half of the page, titled "My Foreign Policy," an oversized Big Pig towering over a group of cringing, diminutive animals, including a beaver, a chihuahua, a lioness, a Gallic rooster, an eagle, and a panda bear, with the caption, "YOU'LL DO WHAT YOU'RE TOLD IF YOU KNOW WHAT'S GOOD FOR YOU!," while, in the background, a large, black, grinning grizzly bear amused himself by swinging on an oversized swing.

Cain and his team liked their chances that, armed with this single piece of paper and with all of the content-and-policy-free images and mental associations it would evoke, Big Pig might be able to wing it for the entire ninety-minute televised presidential debate and maybe even, at key moments, say something unexpectedly sensible and memorable.

Two days later, at Big Pig's first and only televised debate with Henrietta Hen, they were proved correct. With what seemed like genuine conviction, Big Pig blustered and filibustered his way through the entire debate and, for a few seconds at a few key points, offered a moderately persuasive imitation of someone who actually knew something of what he was talking about. Even when Big Pig was talking but not making a lot of sense, he was at least preventing Henrietta from talking and making a lot of sense. And Henrietta had not used on Big Pig the Mark Twain line that Cain had most feared and that neither he nor anyone on his staff had prepared a snappy comeback for: "Big Pig, it's not the things you don't know that worry us–although your vast ignorance is indeed worrisome. It's the things you know *that just ain't so!*"

Silas Cain was not required to throw in the towel at any point during the debate. Big Pig, in not appearing to be a stuttering, drooling idiot with clay arches, had met and exceeded the low expectations Cain and his staff had worked diligently to set.

In the Henrietta Hen camp, several of Henrietta's young hen and geese interns had predicted that Big Pig would "weird himself out of contention" by giving an embarrassingly bad debate performance and Henrietta hoped that they were right. But they were wrong. The media consensus was that, as expected, Henrietta had won the debate on both substance and decorum–but there was also a grudging acknowledgment on Henrietta's team, in the editorial pages, political blogs, and on Twitter and Facebook, that Big Pig had significantly exceeded expectations by not appearing to be a stuttering, drooling idiot with clay arches. Even so, Henrietta remained upbeat and energized. She convened an all-staff meeting for 10 a.m. the next day, so that she could give her charges a final pep talk for the round-the-clock efforts that would be needed in the critical few days remaining.

At 9:59 a.m. the next day, as Henrietta and two of her staffers were filing into the conference room and the meeting was about to start, the campaign's human IT director, Krishna Banerjee, rushed in.

"Henrietta, we've got a *big* problem. Have you checked our website?"

"I looked at it fifteen minutes ago. Why?"

Krishna made a visible effort to compose himself and then blurted out his news. "In the past few minutes, our website has been hacked. There are some very disturbing images on it. I don't know where they came from and I can't erase them. You need to take a look."

Henrietta and her staff pulled out their creature-adapted iPhones and iPads, logged on to www.henriettaforpresident.com, and were aghast at what they saw. The campaign's home page, and every succeeding page, had been wiped clean of any information or internal links describing the campaign. The sole content on the new home page was three, side-by-side images: a doctored photograph of Henrietta swatting Bethany Bee, Animal Farm's most celebrated Queen Bee, with an oversized fly-swatter, above a flashing caption, "When I am President, *I* will be the only Queen at Animal Farm!"; a doctored photograph of a slatternly, winking Henrietta wearing a deep-plunging cocktail dress and fire-engine-red lipstick and facing a long line of roosters, foxes, and coyotes with their tongues hanging out, above a flashing caption, "When you boys get tired of your wives and girlfriends, come and see me!"; and a short video featuring a hen bearing a striking resemblance to Henrietta defecating, one stall at a time, in pig, horse, and cow stalls in some of Animal Farm's largest barns, with an end-of-video voiceover, in Henrietta Hen's unmistakably edgy voice, "I am Henrietta Hen and I approve this message."

"Krishna, pull this stuff down!" Henrietta told him.

"Henrietta, I've tried! Nothing seems to work. I've already called our internet provider and the cyber security experts we have on retainer. The only thing we can do right now is shut down the website until they do their forensic work."

"Do it," Henrietta said curtly. "Meantime, we'll need to send out an email to our entire list of supporters and likely voters and let them know that we've been hacked and that we're taking all necessary steps."

"That's another problem," Krishna said sheepishly. "Our voter and donor lists have been deleted and the group email function doesn't work either. We don't know whether the lists have been shared but, anyway, they are *gone*. And whoever deleted them did a good job covering their tracks."

"What?" Henrietta exclaimed. "So we can't even send out an email blast to our supporters? Krishna, I don't care how you do it or how much it costs or how many people have to be roped in, you *have* to get on top of this and get our website back up and our lists and email access back. Enlist me, or anyone else on the campaign, if you need to. Just get it done!"

Krishna shut down the website and organized a conference call with the campaign's internet provider and cyber security consultants. A series of remote and on-site diagnostic tests were conducted that revealed a large number of highly sophisticated cyber intrusions. Someone had used fake online personas ("Margery Cloud," "William Makepeace," "Joanna Judson"), malicious computer code, and intrusion software called Z-Agent to conduct hacking operations into the campaign's website and into the email accounts of Henrietta Hen, her campaign manager, and the campaign treasurer; unknown persons associated with different fake online personas ("John Waine," "Cathy Witherspoon," "Georgia Tyde") had used a technique known as "spearfishing" to steal the passwords of members of Henrietta's staff and gain unauthorized access to the campaign's donor lists, voter lists, planned advertising buys, and opposition research on Big Pig; standard Microsoft Office functions, such as sending group emails, had been corrupted; and the hackers had also covertly implanted malware onto Henrietta Hen's computer and digital devices that enabled them to capture every key stroke she made and to monitor, in real time, all of her personal and campaign-related emails and text messages.

Whoever was behind these intrusions had expertly deleted event logs, login histories, and computer files in order to cloak their identities. Strangely, embedded in one of the malware programs was a thirty-second video featuring two dozen or so large black bears skating on a frozen pond surrounded by forests and snow-covered mountains, with a sound track that one of Henrietta's raccoon interns–who had recently taken a month's sabbatical from the Juilliard School of Music to work on Henrietta's campaign–identified as a piano sonata in B flat major by the human composer Sergei Prokofiev. The cyber experts had seen pieces of playful mischief and misdirection like this before, in other hacks they had investigated, and paid little heed to it. By 11 p.m., the campaign's website had been restored, the keylog malware on Henrietta's computer and devices had been disabled, the campaign's voter and donor lists had been retrieved (although it was still not known who else might have them), standard Microsoft Office functions had been reactivated, and the campaign's cyber experts expressed guarded confidence that they could repel any future attack.

While Krishna and his team were holed up in a conference room next to the atmospherically-controlled, glass-enclosed space that housed the campaign's web, mail, and file servers, the campaign's phones had been ringing off the hook. Henrietta's precinct captain for the northeast sector called to report that a number of volunteer canvassers had been spurned by voters based on provocative emails and images that had been forwarded to the voters' email addresses earlier that morning. One of the emails purported to be an exchange involving the campaign's married-with-children treasurer to the campaign's married-with-children assistant treasurer, stating, "Henrietta is *so* hot! When this is all over, I'd love to ruffle her feathers!"–to which the assistant treasurer had replied, "Let's make that a threesome!"

Another email purporting to be from Henrietta to her campaign manager proposed that since the number of electoral votes allotted to the foxes and coyotes was larger than the number of electoral votes allotted to the chickens, the foxes and coyotes should be promised that if they helped to elect her there would be "a chicken in every pot." The voters had also been favored that morning with images of Henrietta swatting Queen Bee Bethany with a fly swatter; Henrietta in the deep-plunging cocktail dress coming on to the panting roosters, foxes, and coyotes; and Henrietta relieving herself in Animal Farm's pig, horse, and cow stalls.

The campaign's precinct captains from the southeast and southwest sectors called to report that a new and obscure nonprofit organization calling itself Hens Against Henrietta was sending out doctored images and defamatory tweets about Henrietta to every person with a Twitter account who was listed on Henrietta's donor and voter lists–and that the derogatory tweets were being instantaneously "liked" by everyone who received them and then retweeted to thousands of others. Disparaging comments about Henrietta, her cock husband, and her prior business and political career were metastasizing all over the twittersphere, accompanied by hashtags such as #chickenineverypot, #henpeckedbyHenrietta, #moultypoultry, #HenriettaPlaysChicken, #BanBluePantsuits, and #HenriettaVendetta.

A tweet of disputed origin claiming that Henrietta planned to pay for enhanced music and arts education programs by selling Animal Farm's superannuated cows to human agribusiness interests in Nebraska and Arkansas had also gone viral on the Internet. Reporters from *The Animal Times* called to ask if the campaign wished to make any comment on these developments, in advance of a story the *Times* was planning to publish the next day. And Silas Cain left an angry voicemail on Henrietta's iPhone complaining that Henrietta's emails that morning to some of Big Pig's largest donors, urging them to "Elect Henrietta and make Roast Pork out of Big Pig!" and that "Big Pig is Done–You Can Stick a Fork in Him" were *way* over the line and that, if she really wanted to play that kind of hardball in the final days of the campaign, Cain would gladly oblige her.

When asked whether he or anyone associated with his campaign had had anything to do with this malign cyber mischief, Big Pig denied any knowledge and speculated that perhaps those events were part of a sinister false flag operation orchestrated by Henrietta Hen to make him look bad–or maybe the efforts of some obese, basement-dwelling rooster with advanced computer hacking skills "who really had a hate on for hens."

Big Pig tweeted a prepared statement and also had copies on hand if any member of the traveling press corps might need an extra one:

"As my only comment on this troubling affair–and as a gentleman, it really pains me to say this–perhaps Henrietta Hen is not the dignified, high-class lady she and her team of highly paid publicists have worked so hard to sell to unsuspecting voters."

Although Henrietta suspected that Big Pig was behind the cyber intrusions, she had no evidence of that and was in no position to make unsupported accusations. She knew Silas Cain to be a hard-as-nails but essentially honest campaign operative and thought it unlikely that, even if Big Pig had orchestrated the attacks, Cain had had prior knowledge of them. As Henrietta's team brainstormed on next steps, her campaign manager asked a probing question: even if the campaign could stop the hacks into its website and email systems, how would it know what the cyber hackers might be texting, emailing, or tweeting to voters in the final two days of the campaign and–since the campaign had no way of stopping bogus texts, emails, or tweets to potential voters–what was the best strategy for countermeasures?

Henrietta huddled with her staff. Her key advisors recommended, and Henrietta agreed, that they should divide up the precinct and voter lists and personally visit as many groups of voters as possible. Over the next two days, Henrietta and her hen, geese, duck, raccoon, and turkey aides and volunteers visited virtually every community; reaffirmed Henrietta's core campaign messages of equal educational and economic opportunity for all animals and the importance of Animal Farm's continued international engagement and leadership; and, while being careful not to accuse Big Pig or his campaign, stressed that malicious cyberattacks on the eve of an election were an unfortunate example of the "dirty human politics" to which some animals desperate for power might stoop but which had no place at Animal Farm.

Except during a five-hour period when neither Henrietta nor any member of her staff was getting any emails and texts and somehow every email or text sent to them was being automatically rerouted to email addresses associated with www. theanimaltimes.com, www.animaltimemagazine. com, and www.fakenewsforall.com, her campaign was unable to detect any additional intrusions into its information technology systems. And judging from the enthusiastic voter responses Henrietta and her campaign colleagues were receiving, their eleventh-hour outreaches to voters seemed to be paying real dividends. Bethany, the Queen Bee, was the only key player who was unavailable for a meeting but Bethany's personal assistant assured Henrietta that the Queen Bee was on board.

Although the Animal Farm constitution required that all electioneering needed to stop at 8:00 a.m. on the day before the election, that rule only applied to persons formally associated with a campaign and left open the possibility of private parties championing their favorite candidates right up until the polls closed at 8 p.m. on election day. In prior presidential elections, election day and the day preceding it were typically days like any others, distinguished only by a few horses whinnying about the election over the fences or a few groups of birds chirping about the relative merits of the candidates in tree branches and on roofs and power lines.

But this election was different. Sparked by overheated accusations and counter-accusations about the cyberattacks and the resulting confusion and vitriol, feelings in both camps ran high. Derogatory tweets about Henrietta, retweeted incessantly, rocketed around the twittershere with the hashtags #CrookedHenrietta, #moultypoultry, #SendtheHentothePen, #anycritterbuthenrietta, and #BanBluePantsuits. Henrietta's supporters responded with a plethora of inflammatory tweets about Big Pig, spiced with hashtags such as #IfItWalksLikeaPig, #StickthePig, #nopearlsbeforeswine, #HensRulePigsDrool, and #BigPigLittleBrain.

In a special late edition of *The Animal Times*, the *Times'* social media critic called it "the battle of the hashtags" and wrote that, like the sharply divided public it reflected, the twitter war signified "two angry crowds shouting past each other."

Big Pig spent the day before the election and election day itself playing eighteen holes of golf at Animal Farm's two most exclusive golf courses, one of which–The Big Pig Green Cactus Golf & Wallow

Club–he owned. Silas Cain had suggested that Big Pig prepare both a victory speech and a concession speech, urged that the tone toward Henrietta Hen should be gracious in both speeches, and offered to prepare first drafts. Big Pig thanked Cain for the offer but declined any assistance. Privately, he discounted the need for a victory speech. And as to a concession speech, Big Pig, while slurping beer from a clubhouse trough after his election-day golf round, had worked on a sentence that he believed would showcase his underappreciated class and capacity for graciousness: "Despite our differences, I respect Henrietta Hen and know that, although she may be a bit cracked, a lot of people are saying she is a good egg."

Henrietta's election-eve vigils were more intense and focused. She spent the two days before election day drafting and editing her victory speech and pacing around her expensive manor house located on forty verdant acres a few miles west of Animal House. She didn't need to be told that voters expected the winning presidential candidate to show an element of graciousness toward the loser. But as of 6 p.m. on election day, and notwithstanding several tortuous drafts and redrafts, the most Henrietta could bring herself to say about Big Pig in her draft victory speech was, "Over the past three weeks, I have experienced Big Pig's character first-hand and can truly say, without fear of contradiction, that I consider him to be a very big pig indeed."

On election night, as the returns started to roll in, Big Pig traded ribald stories with his eldest son, Tobias, and some of the campaign staff while he glanced periodically at the television coverage on Faux News. Silas Cain, looking pale and distracted, leaned against a window frame twenty feet away.

To their astonishment, it soon became clear that Big Pig was garnering more votes than anyone had expected and was even, in the breathless commentary of one Faux News pundit, "forging a path to victory."

In a stunning development, early exit polls indicated that many of the hens, vixen, and female coyotes had stayed home (in an apparent expression of protest that reporters were actively investigating) but that the roosters, foxes, and male coyotes, in addition to sheep of both sexes, were voting in historically large numbers and overwhelmingly for Big Pig. *The Animal Times* reported that, according to three reliable sources and contrary to the on-the-record statement she had given to the *Times* only the day before, Queen Bee Bethany had cast her vote for Big Pig and all five electoral votes allotted to the insects would be moving squarely into Big Pig's column. And the cattle vote, which Henrietta Hen's internal polling had always indicated was a cinch to go her way, was closely divided (as one MSNBC commentator gushed, "the cows have *not* come home to Henrietta!")

Upon hearing this news, Big Pig threw his empty bag of potato chips on the floor, took a generous gulp of his Diet Coke, and looked around the room for his wife. "Where's Voluptua?"

Receiving no response, Big Pig stood up on his hind legs and called across the room to Charmayne, the lithe young tigress who was Voluptua's personal assistant. "Charmayne, please go and find Voluptua. She should be *here*, to share in this potentially historic moment!"

Charmayne ambled out of the room, peered into several empty rooms abutting the long corridor of the hotel's penthouse suite, and then nudged open the door to a linen closet just around the corner.

Through the narrow slit of open door, Charmayne observed a sleek leopardess in a prone position, her front paws clasped together, her eyes closed and her head bowed, as if in prayer. A soft flame flickered from a tapered candle just a few inches in front of Voluptua's bowed head.

Charmayne strained to listen without being seen or heard and could just make out Voluptua's fervent, whispered prayer:

"Almighty God and Savior, Lord of all the animals, and of the fishes, and of the insects, and of the winged ones, *hear my prayer*. I beseech You, Blessed Lord, *please, I beg of You, don't let Big Pig win*. Deep down, he knows he's damaged. But he is not evil and he has been a good provider. And if he has a roving eye and sometimes sticks his pecker where it doesn't belong, let *me* deal with him on that. Don't punish him, and the rest of us, by making him president. I know that You are all-seeing and all-knowing, but–on the off-chance You are not–please trust me on this. Big Pig will make a disastrous president. He is vain, impulsive, narcissistic, bullying, even cruel, at times, and is woefully unprepared for the high office of president."

Voluptua paused, drew a deep breath, and dimmed her eyes once more. "Almighty Creator, I have not asked anything from You in all these years–well, maybe just that one time, when You helped me get a special work visa for that lucrative modeling gig I did in New York, a while back, thank You so much for that–and if You grant me this final wish, I promise to be a better Christian, donate even more of my expensive and only gently-worn designer clothes to charity, and somehow make Big Pig, and his sons and daughters, more Christlike too. Immortal Savior, You *must know* the chaos and dysfunction that awaits Animal Farm if Big Pig wins. I again beseech You, for the good of all the citizens and working families of Animal Farm, please don't let that happen."

Voluptua raised her head and looked up distractedly, as if searching for deities on the ceiling. In an even but slightly raised voice, she offered a final, urgent plea: "O Biggest of all Big Kahounas, O Grandest of all Grand Poobahs, *we really need You to cut us a break here!"*

Charmayne reflected on Voluptua's soulful prayer and then tip-toed around the corner and back to the boisterous group, just in time to hear

Big Pig's rant about the criminal charges Henrietta Hen would face if he were elected president. Charmayne told Big Pig that Miss Voluptua was feeling a bit woozy in all of the understandable election night excitement, but would rejoin him and the others presently.

In an elegant, expensively remodeled manor house a few miles away, Henrietta Hen's husband and key advisors wondered where *she* was. While a campaign aide was dispatched to find her, Henrietta could be found outside, near an unlit corner of the house, prostrate and eyes skyward, clucking a heartfelt prayer in terms remarkably similar to the prayer Voluptua had just uttered, including the bit about a husband sometimes sticking his pecker where it didn't belong, but taking a very different view on whether Big Pig was "evil."

These two strong, intelligent, long-suffering women, each propelled by her own combustible mix of ambitions, frustrations, and longings, had prayed for the same divine intervention.

And each woman wondered whether, in the morning, she would still have any faith in whatever gods she prayed to that night.

CHAPTER 7

For more than half the citizens of Animal Farm, the finale of the Big Pig/Henrietta Hen presidential race was a train wreck of smashed hopes, dashed dreams, unanswered prayers, and disquieting fears.

An unlikely combination of the insect vote, the bear vote, the rooster vote, the fox vote, the coyote vote, the sheep vote, the cattle vote, and the pig vote had put Big Pig over the top. In what was universally regarded as one the biggest political upsets in history, animal or human, Big Pig had garnered fifty-one electoral votes, two more than Henrietta Hen, and had won the presidency of Animal Farm.

In Henrietta Hen's camp, there were tears, angry outbursts, and curses of the gods–although at least one woman in Big Pig's camp had cried and cursed the gods too. The election night pundits were all agreed that the shocking result, which neither they nor any opinion poll had predicted, would keep Animal Farm's reporters, political scientists, and historians busy for years. One historian and frequent television pundit, who had written a history of the rise and fall of the pig Napoleon at the original animal farm in England, commented ruefully: "A pig is back in charge, for the first time since Napoleon was ousted in England many decades ago. There is no historical precedent for pig rule at Animal Farm. Only time will tell what that will mean for us."

During the campaign, Henrietta Hen had promised her key staffers and supporters, including her husband, that–not if, but *when*, she became President–they would each be offered a choice post in the Hen Administration (some had even moved from more remote locales and had taken up permanent residence closer to Animal House, in anticipation of that event) or if they preferred to rejoin the private sector, she would help them finesse a soft landing at a well-endowed think tank or leading investment bank. And Henrietta's promises were not confined to others: she had promised herself that, by vanquishing Big Pig in the election, she would expunge her own demons, be able to keep a closer eye on her meandering husband, and earn her place in history as the trail-blazing first female president of Animal Farm.

For his part, Big Pig had promised Voluptua that he could never win and that they would soon regain a measure of privacy and get back to life in the penthouse suite, with their earning potentials enhanced and their personal brands burnished. Silas Cain had given Voluptua the same confident assurances, not only at the inception of Big Pig's campaign but also during an uncomfortably intense private exchange with Voluptua on election night, as the early vote totals were being tallied and the election result still hung in the balance.

Amid all the raucous post-election excitement, recriminations, and prognostications, the pigs at Animal Farm were beyond ecstatic. Big Pig had pulled off the well-nigh impossible. *The pigs were back.* After many decades in the political wilderness, they could now look forward to government actions and policies that would unapologetically advance their interests; roll back the creeping tide of government regulation designed to benefit the undeserving many at the expense of the deserving few; and empower them (in the words of one of Big Pig's most effective campaign slogans) to Take Animal Farm Back Again.

Given Big Pig's woeful ignorance about, and indifference to, government, its conventional processes, and its underlying constitutional norms– and his equally militant ignorance about, and indifference to, the structures and nuances of international relations–Big Pig's advisors and supporters had harbored no illusions about the likelihood that he *would* win the election or, in occasional bursts of private candor, that he even *should* win the election. They were, at their core, hard-bitten realists and disruptors with a shrewd eye for the made-for-prime-time political longshot. Big Pig's presidential run was, for them, an elaborate vanity play which (provided Big Pig didn't get absolutely trounced by Henrietta Hen) would present Big Pig, and them, with a menu of lucrative opportunities in television and in the private sector.

Immediately following the announcement of Big Pig's win, a few of them asked themselves a question to which none of them had given any serious thought: *What the hell do we do now*?

Big Pig, however, was unburdened by ambivalence or uncertainty. The feelings of anxiety and inadequacy that he had occasionally experienced during the campaign had been supplanted by an almost oceanic calm. In the few hours since Henrietta Hen's gracious concession speech, Big Pig had undergone what Silas Cain likened to a Road-to-Mecca conversion.

Big Pig no longer viewed his campaign demagoguery as empty slogans that catered to the whipped-up fears and basest instincts of a carefully targeted segment of voters. Rather, his stunning victory had convinced him that the demagoguery was not, in fact, demagoguery at all. The slogans must be true, he reasoned. Animal Farm did indeed suffer from a dystopian malaise and from a growing number of vexing, intractable problems that only *he*–the Pigster–could fix. He recalled a catchy phrase that Silas Cain had uttered half-jokingly early in the campaign (during Cain's comically unsuccessful attempts to school Big Pig in the rudiments of Western political history): the French King Louis XIV's provocative and short-lived credo, "*L'état c'est moi.*" ("I am the State.")

With the weighty responsibilities of public office

now thrust upon him, Big Pig vowed to live up to his former show name, Colossal Boar, and to stride the political and social media worlds like the modern-day Colossus he was. He would play big on the animal world's biggest stage. He would keep his own counsel and follow his own instincts–for it was those uncanny instincts that had won him the presidency, in the face of withering media attacks and tiresomely repetitive warnings from Silas Cain. He would eschew so-called "expert opinion"–for it was expert opinion that had got the election predictions so spectacularly wrong. And like a Hall of Fame quarterback for a Super-Bowl-Champion football team, he would call his own plays and, when the occasion demanded, change the play at the line of scrimmage and call an "audible" that would confuse and confound his political enemies.

As Big Pig mulled over these heady resolutions, he started to imagine himself in the third person: on the one hand, there was the incomparable, indispensable, larger-than-life Big Pig; on the other, there were the sundry flatterers, toadies, job-seekers, enablers, hangers-on, apologists, factotums, unthinking functionaries, and other smaller-than-life nobodies who, minute-by-minute and sometimes even second-by-second, would judge his moods, praise his far-seeing intelligence, and do his bidding. He conjured up a phrase that captured his vision of Animal Farm under historic pig rule: "Big Pig and a thousand interns."

And at Animal Farm, just as at Big Pig

Enterprises, there would never be any question about who was boss.

Big Pig was still awash in his post-election fever dream when Silas Cain called and asked to see him.

Cain walked briskly into Big Pig's office at the presidential mansion and extended his hand. "Let me be among the first to congratulate you, Mr. President. I look forward to working with you."

Big Pig thanked Cain, patted Cain's hand with his trotter, and offered him a seat across from the imposing, oversized oak desk that had been moved into the presidential office earlier that morning. "By the way, Silas, welcome to 'Animal House.' I just fulfilled my first campaign promise and sent out an Executive Order about the name change, earlier this morning. The new gold nameplates should be installed in the next day or two. My company makes them."

"Yes, I saw the Executive Order," Cain said. "I was hoping, sir, that we could spend some time today sketching out your administration's key priorities for the first month or two. As you and I have discussed, governing is different from campaigning. You need to start telling the citizens–including especially the ones who didn't vote for you–about your plans to make the government more responsive to their needs."

"I must admit," Big Pig gushed, "I'm still giddy from my incredible win over Crooked Henrietta. Nobody saw that coming. Not even *us*, right? Let's ride that for a while."

"Sir," Cain responded, "your election win was indeed impressive. But it was narrow. And though you won the most electoral votes, Henrietta won the popular vote pretty handily. So we need some 'strategic humility' here. Let's start shifting the focus off the election, and off of *you*, and putting the spotlight on all the great things you plan to do for Animal Farm."

"Silas," Big Pig replied haughtily, "I don't accept that Crooked Henrietta won the popular vote. Did you see the cable news coverage this morning? Everyone's saying that a large number of votes cast for the hen were fraudulent."

"Everyone is *not* saying that," Cain replied, as respectfully as he could. "Only a few fringe groups, ones with real axes to grind against Henrietta, are saying that. Those groups have no facts and no credibility. What they are saying is not true. And if you parrot what they are saying, you'll have no credibility either."

Cain knew that Big Pig's sense of his own dignity was immense and that Cain's next comment might bruise it. "Big Pig, I can best serve you by being brutally frank. You have no experience in government. It is really important in these first few weeks, while you're still getting your feet under you, that you at least *appear* to know what you're doing. Let's not stumble right out of the gate, okay?"

Big Pig offered no sign that he had either heard, or agreed with, Cain's point and abruptly changed the subject.

"I glanced at MSNBC's post-election coverage this morning. What's all this bullshit about my having to release my tax returns or disclose the details of my worldwide businesses, or even *sell* those businesses? I said 'No' to that during the campaign. Back then, you told me that might, *your words*, 'be fatal to my candidacy,' remember? And yet, here I am, an elected President. So you'll forgive my skepticism. Let me repeat: my businesses are all family-owned and none of them are publicly traded. It's nobody else's concern how I run them or who I do business with. And just between you and me, I've had some dealings with Bully Bear at Sovietski Farm over the years and know his situation pretty well. Bully Bear has amassed a huge fortune since coming to power at Sovietski Farm. You think that's a coincidence? You think Bully Bear has ever released *his* tax returns or disclosed *his* business interests? I bet he doesn't even *file* tax returns—I mean, who's gonna make him, right?"

Cain squirmed in his chair, bit his lip, and shook his head incredulously. Big Pig sensed Cain's frustration and thought he should make an effort to allay Cain's concerns. Cain could still be useful to him and Big Pig knew that, especially early in his presidency, it might be inconvenient if Cain decided to jump ship before Big Pig was ready to throw him overboard.

"Silas, let me be clear. I just want to wet my snout from time to time. I have no intention of skimming the profits of oil or gas leases, or strong-arming Animal Farm's business leaders into sending me a percentage of their monthly revenues, or demanding kickbacks from contractors who wish to do business here. I'm just talking about continuing to run my businesses while I'm President–and, maybe, you know, giving a little nudge to government policy, here and there, so that the actions we take don't unfairly prejudice me or my family or close friends and don't hit us in our pocketbooks. You think Bully Bear ever restrained himself like that? I mean, that's a *huge* concession. I should get some credit for that. And by the way, whatever happened to the time-honored notion of 'the spoils of office'? That's part of our history and traditions, too, right? I've been in positions of senior management all my adult life. Every new management job has its perks. *Everybody* knows that. What am I not getting here?"

Since early in the campaign, Cain had harbored growing apprehensions about Big Pig's character and fitness for high office but had always managed to suppress them, consoling himself that Big Pig could never win and that his failed presidential run would amount to no more than a footnote or two in the published histories of Animal Farm, perhaps with a brief reference to Cain's role if the election were closer than expected.

But Cain's worst fears were now confirmed: Big Pig had no conception of the real-world implications of his election victory and no intention, or even any capacity to entertain the theoretical possibility, of putting the interests of Animal Farm's citizens, or anyone else's interests, above his own.

As Cain returned Big Pig's steely gaze, he was struck by two depressing thoughts: that he had been instrumental in helping to elect an amoral cipher as President of Animal Farm; and that Big Pig not only was showing early, unmistakable signs of being a bad President–he was intellectually and morally incapable of ever becoming a good President.

And now that Big Pig controlled the levers of presidential power, it could only get worse, Cain knew.

Cain needed time to think and was in no mood to prolong the conversation. He had an idea about how to shorten it. "Okay, let's drop this for now and start thinking about a victory lap. I think another one of your signature barnyard rants is in order. The folks don't get enough of you, in the flesh. And that will help you shore up your electoral base–always a good idea, especially early in a presidency."

"Great," Big Pig replied decisively. "I agree. Let's try for next week, at The Cathouse in the southwest sector, next to the golf course. That's always a fun visit."

Although beneficial ownership of The Cathouse and the luxury golf course adjoining it was cloaked by a complex scheme of dummy holding companies with names like "123 Swing Away Limited," Cain had learned from an anonymous tip a week before the election that Big Pig was the majority owner of both properties. Cain also knew that Big Pig's failure to disclose those facts and Big Pig's presidential direction that the government line his pockets by paying him big fees for the use of facilities he owned was a major ethics issue and that, if reporters from *The Animal Times* and other media outlets ever ferreted out those facts, Big Pig would have a lot of explaining to do.

In Cain's experience, utter shamelessness was a disqualifying liability in a political candidate. But Cain marveled at how Big Pig had transformed shamelessness into a durable competitive advantage. Cain found himself speculating about how Big Pig had broken new political ground here. He quickly arrived at a working hypothesis: if you just didn't know or care about certain things that other people *did* know and care about–for example, ethics in government–your consistent and unapologetic words and deeds, day in and day out, proving that you *really, really didn't care* tended to convince at least some of the voters that they shouldn't care, either, and that corruption in government was just one of life's unchanging certitudes, like the earth's daily orbit of the sun.

Big Pig sensed Cain's uneasiness and favored Cain with a sly wink. "And let's make this Cathouse trip 'staff only'–no wives, daughters, or girlfriends to distract us. There'll be a lot to fit in and the schedule will be tight."

At a strategy meeting the following day, Big Pig

presented Silas Cain with yet another opportunity to test Cain's powers of self-control.

For many years, the two-legged and four-legged citizens of Animal Farm, including Big Pig and the other pigs, had participated in a sensible, grassroots fertilization program under which all the animals agreed to drop their dung directly onto the farm's pastures and ploughlands, at a different spot each day, to save the labor and costs associated with carting manure to and from areas where it was most needed (for reasons never fully explained, the birds declined to participate). If, in a given season, the animals produced more dung than the farm needed, the excess was sold to local farms and the proceeds were contributed to the animals' pension fund.

During Big Pig's campaign—and as part of his core message to voters that, notwithstanding his privileged upbringing and vast wealth, he was a regular down-home pig of the people—Big Pig enthusiastically embraced this practice and video footage of his squatting, public-spirited efforts on Animal Farm's fields and pastures was regularly featured in television campaign coverage and in Big Pig's own slickly-produced campaign videos. And as Big Pig had reminded Animal Farm's voters on countless occasions, he was an astute businessman and shrewd entrepreneur, not a "mere politician" like Crooked Henrietta.

Big Pig saw a real opportunity to showcase as President the bold entrepreneurial thinking he had promised during the campaign.

From a fluff piece on Faux News a few months before, Big Pig had learned about how the CEO of an American luxury car company would occasionally come down onto the shop floor, mix with the garrulous, hard-hatted assembly line workers, and tighten a bolt or two on a few of the cars moving through the assembly line–which cars would then be hyped as Deluxe Presidential Editions and sold at a substantial price premium.

The Faux News piece prompted Big Pig to ask himself a question that haunted him and to which he could give no satisfactory answer: *Why should he give his shit away, since it was "Presidential Shit" and, obviously, worth so much more now*? He wrestled with that question and, after consulting with some of his wealthiest friends and most loyal supporters, convinced himself that, aside from basic issues of fairness and the even-handed protection of property rights, his continued participation in the fertilization program could be interpreted as endorsing communism and might send a dangerous signal to Animal Farm's friends and foes alike.

Big Pig's adult children and other advisors (with one exception) strongly agreed and congratulated Big Pig on his unique capacity for thinking strategically and outside the box. Some of them did request, however, that he consider making exceptions for them as well, so that their own special shit could be packaged, marketed, monetized, and made available to the general public.

Big Pig squelched that idea and called a special

meeting to outline his thinking and chart a path forward.

"Guys," he explained, "I totally get your wish to feed at my trough, now that I am President. And I promise that you'll all have plenty of opportunities to do that. But this is like selling high-end commercial real estate. *Exclusiveness* is key. 'Accept no substitutes,' right? If Animal Farm endorses anything other than Presidential Shit, there may be market confusion or, even worse, market dilution. So I don't want to see any First Family Shit, or any Secretary of State Shit, out there. Only *Presidential* Shit. You all need to keep discharging your patriotic duty and keep doing your dumps in the fields and the pastures, just as before. *Are we clear?*"

Before anyone else could respond, Silas Cain cut in. Cain, the person most responsible for Big Pig's election win, was also the one person in the room who did not hesitate to tell Big Pig what he really thought. "Mr. President," Cain said sarcastically, "with all due respect, you don't shit ice cream. This is a vanity play and will make you look ridiculous. And since you are now the President of Animal Farm, you can no longer afford to look ridiculous. The liberal elites and their fellow travelers in the news media will have a field day with this. Remember our chat yesterday?"

"Refresh my memory," Big Pig answered, bristling at Cain's condescending tone.

"Okay," Cain went on, "let me summarize it for you. The point is, you *won*–and now the media coverage needs to be a lot less about you and a lot more about what you plan to do for the country."

Even after a long and bitter campaign in which he and Silas Cain had frequently shared each other's company, Cain's bluntness and undisguised lack of deference still rankled Big Pig. But he kept a poker face and replied, "Thank you, Silas. I always value your opinion. Please excuse us for a moment."

Cain nodded brusquely and exited the room. After the door was securely shut, Big Pig shrugged and then turned to address the others.

"I love Silas but he's getting a bit wussy. We're going forward with this. Let's have three products. For sale to the public, and as gifts for significant donors, visiting dignitaries, and presidential honorees, I want my dumps to be freeze-dried, scented as needed, cut up into brickettes, and then placed in attractive little boxes bearing the presidential seal and tied with a red-white-and-blue ribbon. There should also be a more expensive, deluxe, 'limited edition' offering, where the presentation box is personally signed by me. The third product will be much more down-market, just my plain turd in a baggie, sometimes with a note attached— for when someone really pisses me off. A number of newspaper reporters come to mind. And for Bright Beaver at Beaverville, maybe we'll mail him a complimentary baggie with my note along the lines of, 'Greetings, Bright Beaver. Here's what we think of your trade policy.'"

The room erupted in shrill laughter and Big Pig's adult children congratulated him on his resourcefulness and peerless cunning.

Big Pig's eldest son, Tobias–who in the past few weeks had taken to referring to himself as Little Big Pig–had an idea. "We're all over it, Dad. But I have a suggestion. When we announce this, let's also announce that you will donate at least ten percent of the after-tax profits from these sales to the animals' pension fund–just so nobody thinks this is all about you."

"Ten percent is a little rich, Tobias," Big Pig said levelly. "It is, after all, *my* shit."

"Okay, Dad, can we say, 'up to ten percent'? That will give us some wiggle room. I mean, 'up to ten percent' could actually mean *zero*, right?"

Big Pig beamed at his eldest son in an avuncular, almost fatherly, way. Particularly in recent weeks, Tobias had shown real promise in applying Big Pig's lessons on how to succeed in business and make, and keep, as much money as possible. "Much better. Thank you, Tobias. Thank you, everyone. Let's get going on this."

Big Pig's executive team sprang into action. Four presidential interns, in back-to-back six-hour shifts, were deputed to follow, quite literally, Big Pig's movements; collect the presidential turds; and then deliver them to a team of technicians located in a secure, undisclosed, climate-controlled room in the basement of Animal House that had previously served as a storage room for presidential memorabilia and had been repurposed to accommodate Big Pig's new initiative.

And though there were initial concerns about adequacy of supply (given the anticipated huge demand), supply turned out not to be a problem. The technicians were relieved to learn that, soon after Big Pig announced his presidential candidacy, he had begun discreetly collecting and freezing all of his feces not needed for campaign photo ops and that several vacuum-packed loads of Presidential Shit would shortly be arriving from a climate-controlled storage facility in El Paso.

Word leaked out about what the four hapless interns were up to and the offices and corridors at Animal House soon abounded in playful riffs on an excremental theme:

"Who *says* 'you can't make this shit up'?"

"Offal, simply *offal!*"

"What a shitshow!"

"Big Pig's *turd* way forward!"

"Little brick shithouse!"

"Presidential Intern Job Description: Taking shit from the President! Chief of Staff Job Description: *Same!*"

When this unbecoming levity got back to Big Pig, he was furious and directed Tobias to ferret out the jokesters and issue immediate pink slips.

Tobias dutifully conducted the review Big Pig had requested. But he quickly concluded that if everyone who had either uttered or laughed at one of these witticisms were fired, there would soon be precious few Animal House employees left to run the government.

So Tobias decided to invoke the four-pronged strategy that he (and his family members and senior Animal House colleagues, including Silas Cain) had learned to deploy when Big Pig issued an idiotic or impracticable order:

Step One, ignore the order;

Step Two, in the unlikely event that Big Pig ever mentions the order again, shrug and claim loss of memory;

Step Three, if Big Pig persists, plead total absorption in executing some *later* order issued by Big Pig (Step Three was tricky, since it made it harder, but by no means impossible, to revert to Step One in connection with the later-issued order); and

Step Four, if all else fails, quickly change the subject (even weeks after the election, reminding Big Pig about his historic, against-all-odds victory over Crooked Henrietta was invariably effective.)

In this instance, as in many later instances, Step One did the trick.

Three days after his key post-election meetings with Cain and Tobias, and with the brickettes and baggies featuring Presidential Shit now selling (as Big Pig privately boasted) "like hotcakes," Big Pig met with Tobias to craft some refinements to the customary oath taken by animals appointed to high government positions at Animal Farm.

Impressed by the exalted sound of it, Big Pig's

daughter, Pigletta, had suggested that the revised oath be called the Porcine Oath and that Big Pig himself should administer it.

The Porcine Oath read:

"I do solemnly swear that I will support and defend Big Pig against all enemies, foreign and domestic, and from any inconvenient provisions set forth in the Constitution of the United State of Animals or other applicable laws; that I will bear true faith and allegiance to Big Pig; that I will well and faithfully discharge the orders issued by Big Pig or by his duly authorized family members and retainers; and that I undertake these obligations freely and without any mental reservation or purpose of evasion. So help me God."

More than his predecessors, Big Pig understood and exploited the power of formal rituals designed to confirm his role as Animal Farm's chief executive without making him appear too pompous or pretentious.

After each oath-swearer recited the Porcine Oath, they were *not* required to prostrate themselves and kiss Big Pig's hoof.

Rather, in an act of grace and ceremony, Big Pig simply lifted his trotter and brought it gently to the oath-swearer's mouth.

CHAPTER 8

Silas Cain knew that his days in Big Pig's administration were numbered.

Cain objected to the Porcine Oath and had declined to swear it. He suspected that this was one presidential directive that neither Big Pig, his eldest son, Little Big Pig (who now bore the title, Special Assistant to the President), nor his eldest daughter, Pigletta (who had also been graced with the title, Special Assistant to the President), would allow him to dodge, particularly since Little Big Pig and Pigletta had themselves sworn the oath. It was common knowledge that, on the rare occasions where Big Pig sought advice at all, he was often persuaded by the last person to speak with him and Cain had, for that reason, finagled an office close to Big Pig's office at Animal House. But Cain found it odd that he had not yet been conferred any title with the new administration and was aware that Big Pig, Little Big Pig, and Pigletta had, in the past two days, scheduled at least three closed-door meetings to which he had been conspicuously uninvited.

Cain determined that when the opportunity next presented itself he would request a private meeting with Big Pig, clear the air, and figure out what role, if any, he could play in helping to shape Big Pig's presidency and, perhaps, prevent some unforced errors and avoidable blunders.

In their closed-door sessions, Little Big Pig and Pigletta advised their father that Cain, having succeeded in getting Big Pig elected, had outlived his usefulness; that Cain's loyalty to Big Pig was conditional, not unconditional, and of a considerably lower order than the filial loyalty Big Pig received from each of them; and that recent press reports detailing Cain's independence from and condescension toward Big Pig–which, they suspected, had been leaked by Cain himself–were bad for the Big Pig global brand and a drag on their father's presidency. Big Pig agreed on all three points and told them that he would let Cain "walk the deck for a few more days and then throw him overboard."

Meanwhile, Big Pig enlisted his new Special Assistants in a number of presidential initiatives. Pigletta was deputed to work with Voluptua on re-decorating Animal House in the profligate, rococo style to which they had all become accustomed, including a new, floor-to-ceiling bay window in the presidential bedroom; new gold toilets, gold bi-dets, gold candelabra, gold nameplates, gold picture frames, and gold plate and utensils, and a 65-inch LED 4K Ultra HD television, with HDR, for each room in Animal House; and, on the back lawn of Animal House, a large, kidney-shaped pig wallow bordered by custom-made paving stones flecked with gold dust.

In a grudging nod to Silas Cain's lectures on the prohibitions against self-dealing by public office-holders, Big Pig instructed Pigletta that, although all of the expensive new gold fixtures and other household items should be purchased from Big Pig Enterprises and paid for out of Animal Farm's treasury, the markup on the purchased items should be no greater than the company's standard 45%– just so nobody could complain that he was taking undue advantage. Pigletta was also urged by Big Pig to get the word out, discreetly and through channels, that his administration would look particularly favorably on those animals and animal nations who chose to continue to frequent the hotels, golf courses, and resorts owned by Big Pig Enterprises, whether at Animal Farm or elsewhere in the United States and abroad, and that administration officials would be "keeping book" on who was following, and not following, that sound advice.

Little Big Pig was given three priority tasks: to lease from Big Pig Enterprises, for presidential business and at the company's usual corporate rates, two helicopters and to have each one repainted red-white-and-blue to achieve "a more American look" and in deference to the future business Big Pig hoped to transact with the United States government (for many years, each helicopter in the Big Pig Enterprises fleet had been painted royal blue but Big Pig had determined that blue was "a Henrietta Hen color" and should be expunged from Animal House and other government installations); to second the top graphic designers from Big Pig Enterprises, put them on the government payroll, and task them with creating designs for a new Animal Farm flag featuring a silhouette of Big Pig's iconic, dish-shaped face and prominent snout superimposed onto the current flag's pasture green background and broken human whip; and to start making arrangements for a military parade featuring the Animal Farm All-Forces Brass Band, five battalions of marching geese infantry, full military regalia, a few short remarks from the incumbent champion of *The Little Pig Bachelorette* TV reality show, and at least one top-of-the-charts female human pop singer who would create buzz and add prestige to the internationally televised event.

In his first presidential interview, with Faux News–which Big Pig had arranged without consulting Silas Cain–Big Pig declared that, being a "very stable genius," his primary consultant would be himself; that he had a good instinct for presidential decision-making; and that he was constrained to consult mainly with himself because he had "a very good brain." When asked whether he thought Pigletta or Little Big Pig also possessed a very good brain, Big Pig replied that, as a father, he loved all of his children and tried not to dwell on whether any of them were in the immediate vicinity when God handed out brains.

As to Silas Cain, Big Pig said that he would always be grateful for Silas's assistance during the campaign and that, in connection with a possible future role for Silas, "we'll see what happens." Big Pig then changed the subject and told the Faux News commentator that, although he had decided to act as his own Treasury Secretary, Secretary of State, Secretary of Defense, and Attorney-General, he did feel the need for a skillful spokespig who could expertly handle press inquiries and help the public understand his bold new strategies for "Putting Animal Farm First."

The day after the Faux News interview, Waffles–a plump, bright-eyed porker who, as communications director for Big Pig Enterprises, had shown real adroitness in deflecting reporters' questions about Big Pig's sundry liaisons with women not his wife–was announced as the official presidential spokespig. Like her boss, Waffles aspired to play on a bigger stage and, in lobbying Big Pig for the role, shrewdly chose flattery as her weapon of choice. After learning from Pigletta that "the new president" was in need of a press secretary, Waffles had requested an audience with Big Pig. In remarks she had carefully prepared beforehand, Waffles gushed to Big Pig that, although she did not presume to possess even one iota of his genius as a communicator, she would, if granted the extraordinary privilege of contributing to his legacy, be an avid and loyal student of the Master and always follow his lead.

Big Pig hired her on the spot.

The young porker's name, Waffles, was doubly inspired: by her favorite food, which she garnished with generous dollops of Canadian maple syrup imported from Beaverville (a guilty pleasure that Big Pig also shared); and by her ability, while skipping amiably from side to side and whisking her curly tail, to obscure and deflect questions from the press about the veracity of Big Pig's tweets and other public statements.

Waffles proved to be highly effective in her new role. Her ability to dissemble, seemingly effortlessly, in front of a large group of openly skeptical reporters earned her high marks from Big Pig, who privately told Pigletta, "I love Waffles. I mean, who else would do this job, and do it so convincingly?"

When Big Pig insisted—in the face of overwhelming photographic evidence to the contrary—that his inauguration was attended by the largest number of animals ever to attend a presidential inauguration at Animal Farm, Waffles noted that Queen Bee Bethany had attended Big Pig's inauguration and that, because the Queen Bee had cast all of the electoral votes on behalf of countless millions of insects living at Animal Farm and had cast them in Big Pig's favor, her presence at the inauguration was tantamount to those countless millions of insects having been present at the inauguration too.

At the end of her first week as presidential spokespig, Waffles began her press briefing with tears streaming down her plump cheeks as she extolled Big Pig's wisdom, the profound goodness in his heart, and the abiding love he bore all animals everywhere–even and especially the unfortunate animals who lived under despotic human or animal rule elsewhere–and declared that Big Pig's ascension to the presidency of Animal Farm USA was being heralded, worldwide, as a beacon of hope.

Responding to this and other cringeworthy performances, *The Animal Times* published an editorial titled, "The Lies That Bind":

"Waffles, the President's spokespig, is well-named. Unlike the pig minister of propaganda at the original animal farm in England, Waffles does not attempt to turn black into white. Rather, she imperturbably responds to questions that call for black or white answers either with outright falsehoods or with statements that are muddy, muddled shades of gray–which responses, in turn, cause the questioners to wonder why they even bothered to ask. In an administration where the facts and the truth, once ferreted out, spark public outcry and government embarrassment, Waffles performs an essential function for her truth-challenged boss. *Our* essential function, in the free and independent press, is to make sure that Big Pig, Waffles, and other government officials do not play us for the fools they evidently think we are."

Although it should have come as no surprise to Big Pig–he had won an electoral college victory by a razor-thin margin, had lost the popular vote

to Henrietta Hen, and had alienated vast numbers of citizens with his bombastic, misogynistic,
take-no-prisoners campaign–Big Pig was surprised
and angered by the negative press coverage and
blamed Silas Cain for it. Big Pig was incensed
by Cain's refusal to embrace and proselytize the
post-election theme that Big Pig, Little Big Pig, and
Pigletta had come up with in one of their closed-
door sessions: namely, that Big Pig and his adult
children, like the members of Animal Farm's military, *were also making large sacrifices for their
country* because they couldn't possibly make as
much money holding government office as they
would have made had they remained in the private
sector and selfishly let the country be taken over
by Crooked Henrietta and her gang.

It was time for Cain to get the proverbial shove
overboard, Big Pig had decided–but not quite yet.
There were still three tasks for which Cain's connections and skill set would come in handy.

In their daily coverage of Big Pig, reporters
and columnists had begun to salt their submis-
sions with derogatory expressions that put pigs in
general, and Big Pig and his adult children in particular, in an unflattering light. Big Pig demanded
that the word go forth–but not from him–that the
continued use of any of those expressions would
result in the news organizations whose employees
wrote or uttered them being barred from all future
Animal House press briefings and presidential access. Cain agreed to help Big Pig compile the list

but declined to be the one to pull a heavy on the Animal House press corps, so Waffles was foisted with that duty.

The list of forbidden expressions included: "eats/squeals/snorts/sweats like a pig"; "oink," including the expression, "everything but the oink"; "pigs at the trough"; "as happy as pigs in shit"; "saved his/her/their bacon" or "bacon-save," as in "That was a major bacon-save!"; "go the whole hog"; "high on the hog"; "hog-tied"; "in a pig's eye"; "pig pickin'" or "pig pickins"; "Let's put some lipstick on that pig!"; "male chauvinist pig"; "pig ignorant"; "as graceful as a pig on ice"; "pig in a poke"; "pig out"; "pig sty"; "make a pig of yourself"; "road hog"; "make a silk purse from a sow's ear"; "grunt work"; "ham it up"; and "hog wild."

Silas Cain curated the list and had some fun by adding a few of his own personal favorites, including "Yum, yum, pig's bum!"; "Even a blind pig finds an acorn once in a while"; "The pig is in the parlor"; "He'll go far if the little pigs don't eat him" (namely, if nothing gets in his way); "Cast not your pearls before swine"; "We've still not kept pigs together" (we don't know each other well enough to drop formalities); and "Every pig has his St. Martin's Day" (in Spain, November 11th, St. Martin's Day, is the traditional day when human pig farmers slaughter fattened pigs in preparation for winter.)

Waffles dutifully notified the Animal House press

corps and published the list on Animal Farm's official government website.

Reflecting on the daily drumbeat of negative media coverage in the first few weeks of his presidency, Big Pig formed a number of conclusions. First, that he needed to "go big," and quickly, on a few key initiatives tied to the campaign promises he had made to his rabid electoral base. Second, that getting the President of Casa Chihuahua to agree to pay for the promised wall along Animal Farm's southern border, and getting the young upstart Prime Minister of Beaverville to eat some dirt on longstanding trade issues between Animal Farm and Beaverville, would be hailed as early, "big" successes. Third, that Silas Cain's extensive contacts with political leaders at Casa Chihuahua and Beaverville would be useful in achieving those two desired outcomes and turning the news cycle in a more positive direction.

And finally, out of an abundance of caution, Big Pig thought it would be prudent to engage a food taster and added that item to Pigletta's priorities list. (Big Pig had someone in mind for the role. A few days after the election, an ambitious young pig intern named Jerome had caught Big Pig in the hallway of Animal House and gushed that, in addition to the many other blessings conferred by Big Pig's election, Jerome's girlfriend had told him that his lovemaking techniques had improved dramatically since election night and that even the water tasted better now, thanks to Big Pig's inspirational leadership. Jerome's fellow interns had graced him with a nickname, Toady. Big Pig advised Pigletta that Toady–assuming he wasn't poisoned in the line of duty–was the stuff of which assistant press secretaries are made and to please make a note.)

Big Pig instructed Cain to set up calls with Maximo Poocho Chihuahua, the President of Casa Chihuahua (whom everyone called "Moocho") and with Bright Beaver, the newly-elected Prime Minister of Beaverville, and requested that Cain be present on both calls so that they could compare notes afterwards.

Casa Chihuahua, the animal nation sponsored by the Republic of Mexico soon after the establishment of Animal Farm USA, shared a relatively porous thirty-mile border with Animal Farm. The majority of animals who resided there were chihuahua dogs who eked out a subsistence living by working on small, family-owned farms or by taking low-wage jobs in the animal nation's antiquated lumber mills and rundown manufacturing plants. For many years, male chihuahuas of all ages had crossed the border in search of better-paying jobs as farm laborers, farriers, blacksmiths, handymen, carpenters, tree-cutters, masons, plumbers, electricians, and oil riggers, and as gardeners, security guards, and wait staff at Animal Farm's hotels, resorts, and golf courses, and a few had brought their families with them or started new families and ultimately acquired citizenship.

The migrant chihuahuas who worked at the

farms, manufacturing plants, hotels, and oil rigs and refineries were overwhelmingly law-abiding and hard-working–indeed, so much so that their Animal Farm employers invited them back year after year.

During the Sage Raven and Crafty Coyote administrations, the growing influx of chihuahuas from south of the border had been augmented by chihuahuas and other dog and animal breeds making the long and often dangerous trek north from Guatemala, El Salvador, Honduras, Colombia, and other Central and South American countries to escape grinding poverty, repressive government regimes, and the violent criminal gangs, animal and human, that trafficked in kidnapping and prostitution and plied the immensely profitable worldwide trade in heroin and cocaine.

The two prior administrations had set up an imperfect but reasonably workable immigration scheme under which employers could sponsor, either temporarily or permanently, foreign animal workers for employment within Animal Farm; foreign animals seeking asylum, on the grounds of demonstrated government or gang-related persecution in their home countries, would be given a fair chance to present their legal claims; and animals who were ultimately denied entry, either because no domestic employer would sponsor them, the labor market could not absorb them, or they could not present sufficient evidence justifying a grant of asylum, would be treated decently at Animal Farm expense while their immigration cases were pending.

In a one-page memo that Cain had prepared for Big Pig in preparation for the call with Moocho Chihuahua, Cain made it clear, in the first sentence, that the current size and mix of foreign animals seeking lawful entry into Animal Farm–including from Casa Chihuahua and from human nations south of the border–was no greater or more threatening than had been the case under the two prior administrations and that, given the overall growth in the domestic economy in the twelve months preceding Big Pig's election, granting work visas, permanent residence, or asylum to foreign animals in numbers comparable to prior years would reflect merely sustainable growth in Animal Farm's workforce and overall population. In the memo's second sentence, Cain put the chances at zero that Moocho Chihuahua would agree to pay for a border wall and that Big Pig should stop talking about the wall and work with Moocho to help bolster Casa Chihuahua's domestic economy, which ultimately would lead to fewer of its citizens being forced to uproot their lives in search of a better life elsewhere. The third sentence of Cain's memo, still "above the fold," explained that Animal Farm and Casa Chihuahua had enjoyed a long and mutually advantageous relationship that had enriched the citizens of both nations and Big Pig should heed that fact in his introductory call with Casa Chihuahua's president.

But with Big Pig's having succeeded in whipping up his resentful, credulous, middle-class electoral base into believing that whatever economic woes and other life disappointments they and their offspring faced were attributable, not to the unevenly distributed benefits of globalization (which neither his administration, nor any prior administration, had successfully tackled) but to "radical chihuahua terrorists," "foreign-born rapists," and assorted "other lowlifes from shithole countries who don't look like us," acknowledging Cain's points was not an option.

Big Pig sternly reminded Cain that he had promised his supporters a wall, a *massive* wall, along the southern border and that he expected Cain to help him persuade Moocho to issue a public statement confirming that Casa Chihuahua would pay for the wall. He told Cain to get Moocho on the phone so that the two of them could, in Big Pig's blunt vernacular, "put the little chihuahua's mind right."

The call with Moocho Chihuahua did not go well. As Silas Cain had predicted, Moocho told Big Pig that there was "zero chance" that Casa Chihuahua would agree to pay for any border wall and that Moocho and his fellow countrymen considered the very idea a grievous insult. Big Pig was surprised by Moocho's vehemence and resolve, exclaiming, "Hey, Moocho, I made the wall one of my core campaign promises and if I don't deliver on that it will make me look weak and a bit of a dope," to which Moocho replied levelly, "Señor Presidente, as we sometimes say in our country, 'that pig has already left the sty.'"

The call rolled quickly downhill from there, with Big Pig threatening to close Animal Farm's southern border entirely if Moocho didn't immediately reverse course and with Moocho ending the call by telling Big Pig that a border closure would dangerously escalate tensions between the two countries and that Big Pig would do well to remember that Casa Chihuahua and other nations south of the border had lots of birds too.

After Moocho hung up on him, Big Pig's prominent pink snout twitched aggressively. "You were not helpful on that call, Silas. And what did Moocho mean by the 'birds' comment. Is this guy a birdbrain, or what?"

"That may well be, Big Pig," Cain answered, stifling a sneer. "Let's put Casa Chihuahua on hold for the moment and try to engage with Beaverville. Have you reviewed my memo?"

"What memo?" Big Pig asked curtly, still vexed by Moocho's unabashed refusal to do his bidding.

"The bottom half of my one-page memo to you–the one you're holding," Cain replied.

The bottom half of the one-page memo Cain had prepared for Big Pig (the top half dealt with Casa Chihuahua) explained, also in three crisp sentences, that Beaverville was one of Animal Farm's most trusted allies and most important trading partners; that it had just elected an articulate young Prime Minister, Bright Beaver; and that the two animal nations had always negotiated, in a friendly and fact-based way, their sometimes fractious bilateral trade disputes and that Big Pig should follow his predecessors' sensible lead.

"I didn't get to that part," Big Pig said. "Anyway, let's do the call. I know what I need to say."

"Big Pig," Cain interjected, "earlier this morning, I got a nasty call from Beaverville's Foreign Minister asking why you sent Bright Beaver a bag of shit, along with a note signed by you on Animal House stationery saying, 'Greetings, Bright Beaver. Here's what we think of your trade policy.' He also demanded that you issue an immediate public apology. I told him that I had no idea what he was talking about, but would inquire. Did you really send a bag of shit to the leader of our closest ally in the western hemisphere? *Please* tell me you didn't do that."

Big Pig remembered the chuckles he, Little Big Pig, and Pigletta had shared in speculating about who, in the Animal Farm press corps and at the capital cities of various foreign governments, should be presented with a newly-minted bag of presidential shit and also remembered Little Big Pig's uncharacteristically astute comment, "That's why they call it a 'shit list,' right, Dad?" And though Big Pig was (as best he could remember) only joking at the time, he concluded that Little Big Pig must have taken him literally and actually sent a bag of turd to Beaverville's new prime minister.

"Silas," Big Pig said, in the most soothing tone

he could muster, "that was an unfortunate misunderstanding. Just go ahead and apologize to Bright Beaver on my behalf and we'll start the trade talks with Beaverville once the apology has been delivered and accepted."

"*You* need to apologize, Big Pig," Cain replied. "This is your, and your family's conduct, not mine. I don't make a habit of apologizing for other people's blunders–not even for presidents."

Big Pig's pink face assumed a surly scowl. For the second time in ten minutes, he'd been thwarted by functionaries whose assigned role was to do his bidding. "Silas, you work for *me*. You and I need to come to an understanding. You don't get to pick and choose the tasks I assign you. Are we clear?"

Cain was relieved that the "come to Jesus" moment with Big Pig had finally arrived. He sensed that the next few minutes would be his last act in this weird morality play featuring arriviste pigs in all the leading roles. And he vowed, before the final curtain fell, to get some things off his chest.

"Big Pig, I agree that we need to reach an understanding. I have tried my best to serve you. Having worked hard to get you elected president, I want you to succeed. But you are traveling a dangerous road. I have some advice for you, if you care to hear it."

"I'm listening."

Cain leaned forward. "I have high-level contacts in the American intelligence community and I know for a fact that Bully Bear and others at Sovietski

Farm were behind the cyberattacks that took place just before your election win. For reasons of their own, the Americans are staying mum about that. But at some point it will become widely known. My professional reputation is valuable, at least to me. Politics is not bean-bag and I play the game hard. But I don't cheat. So I need to ask: what do *you* know about Bully Bear's involvement?"

"I don't know anything about it," Big Pig replied stiffly.

"That's not what my American contacts tell me," Cain said, "but no matter. Here's my advice: Bully Bear plays rough–*very* rough. His flame blows red hot and you don't want to get burned by it. There's a wise proverb, Big Pig. If you sup with the devil, you had better carry a *long spoon*."

Big Pig's tail became hard and straight and then twitched sharply from side to side, a rare but unmistakable sign that he was engaged in intense mental activity. "Anything else?"

Cain was tempted to confront Big Pig with the shameless self-dealing and conflicts of interest in which Big Pig and his adult offspring had engaged since the election–to tell Big Pig that his conduct in office demonstrated "filling the trough" rather than "draining the swamp" and that what used to be called gross corruption Big Pig now practiced openly, without disguise and without reproach. But Cain resisted the temptation. He had bigger fish to fry.

Climate change, although not the subject of any

campaign promise by Big Pig, had resurfaced as a major issue following publication of comments Big Pig had made to a couple of major donors the week after his election. At a private reception held after one of Big Pig's post-election victory laps, he had told two wealthy campaign donors, both of whom were CEOs of multinational oil companies that held lucrative drilling rights at Animal Farm, that they had nothing to worry about on that score. Big Pig reassured them that he was against pressuring the humans to curb their greenhouse gas emissions because that might lead to a ban on the aerosol hairsprays he had used since boyhood to make himself irresistible to the ladies.

Predictably, *The Animal Times* and other news and social media outlets had a field day with that scoop (one widely-read blog was titled, "Grooming a Pig President, the Planet be Damned") and Big Pig and his metrosexual grooming needs became the butt of every standup comedian and late-night television host and also sparked loud and militant protests from animal rights and human environ-mental groups on every continent.

"Big Pig, you need to address climate change, if only to preserve your standing as president. The birds and the other animals are livid about your hairspray comments. Please remember that combating climate change is, for them, an exis-tential question. Recall your history. It was the Creature Insurrection, led by the birds many de-cades ago, that caused Animal Farm USA to come into existence. The birds and animals that rebelled once are apt to rebel again, if provoked."

Big Pig was skeptical. He had not yet paid any real price for following, as president, the venal and racist instincts that had got him elected in the first place and saw no reason to change now. "I'm sticking to the history *you* taught me, Silas. 'La tat sest moy.'"

Cain shook his head in disbelief. "I think you mean, *'L'état c'est moi.'* And Big Pig, the last French king who embraced that philosophy sparked a bloody revolution and had his head chopped off, as did his wife. So I'd be careful about that one."

"That was then and this is now," Big Pig replied sharply. "I side with Henry Ford: 'History is bunk.' So where are we, Silas? Are you going to go along with me in the things I have to do? You need to decide: are you in, or *out?*"

In working with Big Pig over the past several weeks, Cain had noticed that the tried-and-true, four-step program that he and others had used to avoid following one of Big Pig's idiotic orders also worked when Big Pig asked a question you couldn't, or didn't want to, answer. Cain abruptly changed the subject.

"Getting back to the Bright Beaver situation, I think that once you apologize to Bright Beaver we can get our trade issues with Beaverville sorted out. At some point, Big Pig, you're going to need some friends in the animal democracies and there's been no greater friend to us than Beaverville. Making nice with Bright Beaver would be an excellent place to start."

Cain's strategy worked. Big Pig forgot about his ultimatum to Cain and focused instead on his virulent dislike of Bright Beaver, the newly-elected Prime Minister of Beaverville who had made no secret of his distaste for Big Pig's ultra-nationalistic, xenophobic, anti-immigrant campaign rhetoric and had declined to make the customary courtesy call congratulating Big Pig on his election victory. Many of Big Pig's most loyal supporters privately acknowledged that Bright Beaver–who had become Prime Minister of Beaverville only a few months before Big Pig was elected President of Animal Farm–was more fit, more articulate, more charismatic, better educated and, even with his unusually prominent front teeth, better looking than Big Pig.

"That little runt," Big Pig bellowed, "is getting too big for his britches. Maybe we should slap some new tariffs on the lumber and building supplies Beaverville exports to us. Let Bright Beaver and his buck teeth chew on *that!* And what's *his* net worth, anyway? How many females has *he* bedded?"

For Cain, that did it. If tasteless, idiotic remarks were straws, that last tasteless, idiotic remark was the straw that broke the camel's back. Cain knew that his reply would mark the end, but he was okay with that. In fact, he looked forward to the end and marveled that it hadn't come sooner. He'd seen enough vulgarity, mendacity, and executive stupidity from these pigs–enough to last a lifetime. "On the adultery and fornication fronts, Big Pig, he's definitely not in your league–but to be fair, no one else is either. You're in *a league of your own*, no question."

Big Pig glared at Cain for several seconds while his snout twitched aggressively from side to side. "You're fired. Get out!"

Cain got up from his chair and, with considerable dignity, left Big Pig's office without uttering a word.

A few minutes later, Big Pig tweeted:

"When I launched my presidential campaign, I said that Cain is Able. But Silas Cain has been disloyel and unprofessional and a few minutes ago I fired him. So let me ammend my earlier tweet: CAIN HAS BEEN DISABELED! LOL"

Fifteen minutes later, Big Pig tweeted this news again, with the only three changes being corrections to the misspellings of "disloyal," "amend," and "disabled." The "LOL" was still there.

Cain felt that he owed a call to Barrington Beaver, Beaverville's Foreign Minister, to confirm his dismissal as a member of Big Pig's administration. Barrington expressed his regrets and then told Cain that, unless Bright Beaver got his public apology, there would be no trade talks between the two nations and maybe Beaverville would stop exporting to Animal Farm the specially-designed pig condoms (made from recycled hockey pucks) that Big Pig and his pigster friends had been buying in bulk for many years and which only Beaverville produced, and also stop exporting the Canadian maple syrup that Big Pig and Waffles so coveted. The two seasoned political hands had a good laugh over that and resolved to stay in touch.

Big Pig called an emergency meeting with Little Big Pig and Pigletta. The three of them met in the secure conference room next to Big Pig's presidential office. Big Pig briefed them on the Moocho Chihuahua call and on Cain's dismissal. He then told them that he had been working on an idea that they needed to hold in strict confidence—an idea that might well make his presidency by killing three birds with one stone: getting the border wall built; getting the Mexican chihuahuas to pay for it; and cementing his base, and possibly even guaranteeing his re-election, by protecting his core supporters from the foreign hordes who were threatening their livelihoods, making the nation's pastures, barns, and streets unsafe, and polluting Animal Farm's gene pool.

As his two adult offspring listened attentively, Big Pig reminded them that the phrase "back off" was not in his vocabulary and that the secret of his extraordinary success in business and, more recently, in politics, was that when more timid souls folded, he *doubled down*. Moocho Chihuahua's refusal was a life lesson for them: it required that they double down on the campaign promise of building the border wall. Backing off was not an option.

Big Pig explained that his idea for getting the border wall built was inspired by the expensive violin lessons Little Big Pig and Pigletta had received from an early age–and how, in teaching them the violin, the human violin teacher had used a variation of the so-called "Suzuki method." Under that method, Pigletta and Little Big Pig were first provided with very small violins and bows appropriate to their small size and, as they grew older, bigger, and more technically capable, the size of the violins and bows they were given to practice on were also corresponding larger until they both became old enough to handle regularly-sized string instruments.

Pigletta and Little Big Pig were perplexed by their father's comments and wondered whether he had momentarily lost it. But they knew that there was almost always a point at the end of one of their father's screeds and determined to hear him out.

Big Pig told them that, going forward, the government would show "zero tolerance" toward any chihuahua or other noncitizen seeking entry into Animal Farm and that, if a noncitizen entered the territory seeking a work visa or seeking asylum, he or she would immediately be detained for further processing. Claims for asylum, for work visas of any sort, and for permanent residence or citizenship would no longer be granted absent a specific order from the President of Animal Farm. Noncitizen animals who sought entry and were accompanied by family members would be put into one group, the "families" group; and noncitizens animals who sought entry and were *not* accompanied by family members would be put into a second group, the "individuals" group.

The families group would then be further divided, with the parents being physically separated from their children. All of the animals in the families group, young and old, parents and children, would be given a combination physical fitness and rudimentary intelligence test to determine their suitability for skilled manual labor. The animal parents who passed that test would be given a choice: agree, as part of a work crew that would also include their detained children, to help build the border wall along the length of Animal Farm's southern border with Casa Chihuahua; or refuse and face deportation–and be separated, indefinitely and perhaps forever, from their detained children.

Taking a leaf from the Suzuki method, Animal Farm would provide each detained adult, teenager, and child who passed the fitness and intelligence test and who agreed to help build the border wall with an appropriately-sized saw, hammer, screwdriver, ladder, tape measure, construction helmet, and other construction tools and materials; with expert instruction in the use of them, at no cost to the detainee or his family; and, for the duration of their service to Animal Farm, with free accommodations near their assigned construction site.

The noncitizen animals who did not pass the physical and intelligence test or who refused to help build the border wall would themselves be separated into two groups: parents, and everyone else. The parents would be swiftly deported to their home country. Their children would either be put up for adoption by an animal family living at Animal Farm or sold as pets to humans living in Texas, New Mexico, Oklahoma, or elsewhere in the United States.

Finally, the program would also make allowance for able-bodied noncitizen animals seeking work visas at Animal Farm who were not accompanied by a family member to be granted work visas at the President's discretion–so that the business community would have no reason to complain that the new "zero tolerance" immigration plan would disrupt the workforce needs of Animal Farm businesses.

As Big Pig saw it, the genius of his plan was that the border wall would get built by the very animals it was intended to keep out and Big Pig could crow to his base that, for all intents and purposes, the chihuahuas would pay for it.

Big Pig advised Little Big Pig and Pigletta that, at least until the wall-assembly plants and detainee accommodations were up and running, it would be best if the plan were kept as confidential as possible and not communicated through an Executive Order. If word leaked out, Waffles would stand ready to proclaim the program as a win-win for all concerned: the urgently-needed border wall would be built, on time and under budget; the chihuahuas would, in a very real sense, "pay for it"; the program would become a poster child for the core Animal Farm values of selfless public service and the dignity of work; the workforce needs of Animal Farm's business community would be safeguarded; and, as a bonus, chihuahuas and other foreign animals, young and old, would be taught useful trades which, when the border wall was completed, they could use to good advantage in their home countries.

And if, under this program, large numbers of noncitizen chihuahuas and other foreign animal parents and their children suffered lasting trauma by being forcibly separated from one another by order of the government and, for some, even the unspeakable anguish of knowing that they might never again see their parents, children, or siblings, then–in the phrase Big Pig liked to shout out when one of his pigster golfing buddies missed a two-foot putt or drove a tee shot into the water–that was their own "tough titty."

Little Big Pig and Pigletta squealed their approval, extolled the brilliance of their father's plan, and congratulated him on his resourcefulness and peerless cunning.

In thinking through next steps, Pigletta stressed the importance of getting the program's public relations spin and associated terminology just right. She thought it likely that the liberal fake news media would saddle the program with an unfair, derogatory label such as "forced family separations" and call the free accommodations for noncitizen detainees "detention centers," "animal cages," or even "concentration camps." In order to cast the program in its proper light, she recommended that Animal Farm's government use more accurate and less emotive expressions such as "compassionate vocational training" and "tender creature shelters."

Little Big Pig reminded his father and sister that Big Pig Enterprises had a large, undisclosed ownership interest in a company that produced prefabricated "big box" warehouses, steel-reinforced cages, and construction tools of all sizes and descriptions and that he would be happy to negotiate government contracts with that company, select the construction sites along the border, and get the various workstreams started. Given that at least some of the steel-reinforced cages and construction tools would need to be unusually small in order to accommodate newborn chihuahuas and other diminutive detainees, Little Big Pig noted that the project would involve a substantial amount of custom fabrication work and that Big Pig Enterprises would profit handsomely from the price premiums associated with that work.

Big Pig beamed at his two children, thanked them for their valuable contributions, and declared that the new immigration plan would be acclaimed not only as the fulfillment of a key campaign promise but also as a demonstration of the bold and decisive presidential leadership that only he could deliver. He ended the meeting by requesting Pigletta to run the communications strategy by Waffles–who, he was confident, would have some clever marketing and public relations insights–and by reminding Little Big Pig that, in any contract for goods or services in connection with this project, the company owned by Big Pig Enterprises should charge Animal Farm no more than it would in a comparable private sector transaction, just so no one could complain that Big Pig was taking undue advantage.

Finally, Big Pig mentioned that the irrigated, tree-studded, five-hundred-acre pasture and grasslands area near the northwest segment of the Animal Farm/Casa Chihuahua border, which for many years had been dedicated as a grazing land and bird sanctuary for superannuated citizens who had reached retirement age, would be well-suited for one of the big box wall-assembly plants and tender creature shelters and that Little Big Pig should feel free to repurpose that pasture, as needed, in the spirit of promoting the larger good.

The next several weeks witnessed a whirlwind of activity along the southern border of Animal Farm. Twelve sites spaced along Animal Farm's thirty-mile border with Casa Chihuahua had been selected as locations for the big box wall-assembly plants and adjacent tender creature shelters; large shipments of powdered grain, potatoes, and milk seconded from the military, construction tools of

all sizes, and industrial grade gas-powered genera-
tors had been transported by truck to each assembly site; wall-assembly plants and steel-reinforced
detainee accommodations and cages were being
constructed and assembled on a round-the-clock
basis; noncitizen detainees who, faced with the
prospect of being separated from their children
for long periods of time, perhaps indefinitely, had
agreed in large numbers to help build the border
wall, working alongside their detained children and
spouses; and makeshift tent cities had sprung up
in various remote locations near Animal Farm's
southern border–whose purpose was to warehouse
noncitizen detainees until either their assigned tender creature shelters were constructed or, in the
case of nonparticipating detainees, until they were
deported, adopted, or sold as pets to humans.

Although there were some rumblings on the
internet and in the news media about these various goings-on, Big Pig, Little Big Pig, Pigletta, and
Waffles had taken extraordinary steps to guard
the secrecy and security surrounding the program
and neither the public nor the press corps had
been able to piece together the larger picture.

As the first group of wall-assembly plants, tender creature shelters, and tent cities neared com-
pletion, the human gardeners at Animal House
noticed an unusual number and variety of birds
flying overhead and intermittently alighting, and
then taking off again, from power lines and tree
branches, but gave the matter no serious thought.

And since learning from Little Big Pig about her husband's bold new immigration initiative, Voluptua had got into the daily habit of taking long, meandering walks around the manicured grounds of Animal House, being careful to avoid the noisy bulldozers, cement trucks, and construction crews assigned to build the kidney-shaped pig wallow that Big Pig had ordered for the back lawn.

With her young son by her side, Voluptua would occasionally pause to admire the grace and precision with which small flocks of birds–some of which were non-native and had never before been seen at Animal Farm–coordinated their crisp take-offs and landings.

CHAPTER 9

Bully Bear settled into his Brazilian oak throne-chair, clasped his massive paws behind his head, and peered at the intricate gold leaf that graced the ceiling of his private study.

After a few minutes, he picked up the phone and summoned Molotov Cocktail.

Molotov strutted in and, as he had done so many times before, leaned his shoulder against the steel-reinforced door and pushed hard with his spindly legs until the door swung shut. After catching his breath, Molotov hopped onto a chair opposite Bully Bear's mahogany desk and, in another well-judged hop, onto the desk itself.

Bully Bear's success in wielding absolute power at Sovietski Farm in the face of the kleptocrats and other political rivals who plotted to dethrone him was attributable to his skill in securing the undivided attention of, and instilling abject fear in, his civilian and military advisors. Office rituals reminding his advisors of just whom they were talking to were, he had found, very effective in setting the proper tone at the top.

Bully Bear closed his eyes, placed his formidable front paws on his desk, and started breathing in an audible, slow-motion rhythm.

From earlier encounters, Molotov knew that his assigned role in this piece of Kabuki theatre was to remain utterly still and quiet until Bully Bear was ready to speak.

At length Bully Bear turned his head to face Molotov, who stood on the desk within one good swipe of the bear's tapered, meticulously-trimmed claws. "Molotov, we need to take measures. It's time to activate our dossier on Big Pig. I take it that the videos we have of Big Pig's exploits in some of the more unsavory precincts of Paris, from a year ago, are still in the vault?"

"Yes, sir–in living color, including the 'Water Works' and 'Golden Showers' cameos where Big Pig really outdid himself. If they gave out Oscars for performances like that, Big Pig would be on *everyone's* short list."

"Good. Please retrieve them, along with the loan documents and personal guarantees Big Pig signed when he refinanced all of his worldwide properties with us. Make three confidential copies of the videos and the loan and guarantee docu-ments. No one else is to know about this."

"Understood," Molotov replied, and then ut-tered the tried-and-true question which, in his long experience with Bully Bear, struck just the right note of focused engagement and cloying defer-ence. "What are you thinking, Leader?"

Bully Bear clenched his two front paws and then relaxed them again. "Big Pig has been a useful idiot for us, no question. The work you and your cyber colleagues did in helping him get elected–against all odds, well done–was successful beyond anything we could have imagined. Just as we had hoped, Big Pig has insulted his allies, weakened their resolve to act against us, sown confusion and division into Animal Farm's politics and popular culture, and hardened its feuding factions–all to our advantage. But it is time for a strategic shift in our loyalties. Big Pig's treatment of the animals seeking asylum has caused an international uproar, including *here*. Yesterday and this morning, I received urgent messages from Moocho Chihuahua, Amelie Eagle, Bright Beaver, Antonia Lyon-Ness, and Li Jun Panda requesting an immediate conference call in order to plan a coordinated, punitive response. Amelie Eagle as much as said to me, 'Hey Bully Bear, we all know you helped get this pig into office–so it's fair that you help the rest of us get him the hell *out* again.' The lady's got spunk, don't you think? I have a grudging admiration for her. Now that Animal Farm's top leadership is in chaos and is an international embarrassment, Amelie Eagle is the unquestioned leader of the liberal animal democracies. She's 'flying high' and gaining considerable praise and prestige in that role, which is not in our interests. Once we get Big Pig taken care of, we'll need to find a way to clip the eagle's wings, too, and bring her down to earth. Start thinking about that."

"Will do," Molotov replied.

"I must admit, I was taken aback by Amelie's call," Bully Bear continued. "Normally, she, Antonia

Lyon-Ness, and the others are on top secret calls plotting to gang up on *me*. Now, they want me to join *them* on a top secret call, so we can all do a gang bang on Big Pig. Politics makes strange bedfellows."

Molotov clucked mischievously. "When you summoned me, I had just got off the phone with the Foreign Ministers from Casa Chihuahua and Beaverville. Both of them insisted that I get your full attention on this and schedule a conference call for later today. They also told me I would soon be hearing from the other Foreign Ministers. I see real opportunity here, Bully Bear, if we act swiftly."

"There's more," Bully Bear said, angrier now. "Some of our most prominent oligarchs–two or three of whom, as you know, want my job and would love to see me falter–have lately grown spines and demanded to know what *I* am going to do about Big Pig. And two nights ago, Katiana ordered me to sleep on the couch and told me there'll be 'no more nooky' until I take decisive steps, this is a direct quote, 'to stop the hateful pig's cruelty.' I suspect that, somehow, Amelie Eagle got hold of Katiana and that the two mothers had a little chat. I won't have this, Molotov! The pig is out of his pen and is shitting all over the place. He's the proverbial useful idiot who has outlived his usefulness."

"I would add another consideration, if I may."

"Go on," Bully Bear replied curtly, still seething that a corpulent pig from another continent six thousand miles away could put his sex life on hold.

Molotov waited a few seconds before responding. "In addition to Big Pig's overreach on the asylum and 'forced family separations' issue, his refusal to do anything to get the humans to address climate change is dangerous for us. The accelerating rate of destruction of bird habitats is creating real havoc in those communities–you've seen the recent bird demonstrations, here and in North America and Europe. From our network of covert agents, we have actionable intelligence that a growing number of militant gull, raven, and other bird factions are forming and that they no longer consider themselves bound by any understandings we, or the other animal nations, have with the humans. If we don't take steps to address these open sores and somehow get Big Pig out and get Animal Farm back into the international fold, I fear that our bird and animal brothers will revolt and declare a pox on all our houses, including *yours*. I am not confident we could survive that."

Bully Bear clenched his fists and leaned even closer. "Molotov, we have misjudged this pig. We are no angels–we can admit that, at least to ourselves. But whatever else we do, we do not separate mothers from their little children or inflict cruelty on babies, as a matter of government policy or simply 'because we can.' First and foremost, we are *men*. We will never shame ourselves like that. And we need to ask ourselves: if this pig is capable of *that*, what else is he capable of? Enslaving the little critters and their parents, training them for careers in hospitality, and making them work for free at his hotels and golf resorts? Making them fill sandbags for when the rising oceans–thanks, in no small part, to Big Pig's denial of climate change–start flooding the coastal areas and gushing into the lobbies of his five-star hotels?"

"Sage Raven and Crafty Coyote were thorns in our sides, to be sure," Molotov interjected. "But at least their moves and countermoves were rational and somewhat predictable."

"With Big Pig," Bully Bear added, "it's chaos on stilts, daily, and of an increasingly malevolent sort. How long before he trains that chaos and malevolence on *us*?"

Molotov remained silent, rightly surmising that no response was required.

Bully Bear leaned back in his throne-chair. "There is much to consider."

"We need to talk to this pig," Molotov urged. "Give him a reality check."

Bully Bear scratched his chin. "We need to do much more than that. I have been thinking."

"What are your thoughts, Leader?"

"Molotov, let it be known to Big Pig, through channels, that we would be honored to receive him here, as his first official state visit, to kick off a new era of cooperation, peace, and understanding between our two kingdoms. Make sure to use the word 'kingdoms.' Big Pig will *love* that. Tell him we wish to honor him with an all-services military parade–I understand he loves parades–and to present him with the Proletarian Medal of Freedom, our highest civilian honor and which has never before been awarded to a foreign national. Tell him that, as we speak, ten battalions of our elite geese infantry are marching on Potemkin Parade Ground, honing their goose step, in preparation for the televised parade we will give in his honor. A lavish state dinner, with cheeseburgers and all of Big Pig's other favorite dishes, will also be on the first-day agenda. Finally, tell him there is a three-hundred-acre plot of forest and rich pasture bordering the Shashka River that we think would make a great luxury golf course and resort and that we'd very much value his expert opinion, and will pay him handsomely for it."

"And if he wavers," Molotov added, with a twinkle in his eye, "we'll tell him that we will of course make available, *very* discreetly, some of our most skilled and alluring leopardess and sow sex workers and that we'll schedule the extracurricular activity for the second day of his visit, while Voluptua and Katiana spend the afternoon checking out the new chinchilla fashions along Four Paws Promenade."

"Good. Definitely tell him that too."

"What should we propose as agenda items for the working group?"

"Don't worry about an agenda, Molotov. There won't be any 'working group.' Agree to any items Big Pig or his advisors want. It won't matter, in the end."

"Apologies, Leader, but I do not understand."

"*Molotov Cocktail, try to keep up with me!* It

won't matter because, after the parade and the presentation of the Medal of Freedom, we'll have Big Pig and his advisors for dinner–and maybe for breakfast too. Every pig has his St. Martin's Day."

"Now I understand," Molotov replied, having caught the sinister drift of Bully Bear's remark. "What shall we do about the leopardess?"

"Let the leopardess keep her spots. As I said, we don't make war on mothers or their little babies. It is the guilty *fathers* who must be made to pay." Bully Bear peered down at his belly and began rubbing it playfully with his long, razor-sharp claws. A chilling grin broke across his fearsome grizzly face. "Yum, yum, pig's bum!"

Molotov jumped up and down on his spindly legs and congratulated Bully Bear on his resourcefulness and peerless cunning.

Just then an idea occurred to Molotov. He well knew that, once Bully Bear had decided on a course of action, it was perilous to suggest an alternative one. But on quick reflection, Molotov decided to risk it. The idea was too important not to share.

"Leader, Big Pig needs to remain alive, at least until he repays the large sums he owes us. There may be another, and faster, way to achieve our objectives–and one where your paw prints are not all over it."

Bully Bear shot Molotov a stern look. "And that is?"

"*Remember the Birds!*"

"Interesting, Molotov. How would that work?"

"We could mobilize very quickly. The birds and animals here and on the other continents are in a rebellious mood and are close to acting unilaterally. We should tell them that we want Big Pig out, too, and that we will take care of the planning and logistics and enlist the other animal nations. Over the past few weeks, we have cultivated some workers at Animal House who hate Big Pig with a vengeance and who will shed no tears when he's gone–and will, if we move against him, look the other way. A few of them may even agree to help us. To the outside world, this will look like a spontaneous national insurrection, not an international conspiracy. No 'paw prints.' If you give the order, I will execute it."

Bully Bear fixed his gaze on a small crack in the gold-leaf-gilded ceiling and remained silent for a few seconds. "Good, Molotov. Coordinate with Amelie Eagle and the others. Tell them you are acting on my express authority, that we all need to take steps to ensure deniability, and that any of them can reach out to me in private, as needed. Once the plan has been fleshed out, I'll want a full briefing. What timing do you propose?"

"We should be able to execute in the next few days, if everyone plays his part," Molotov replied. "I will check back in a couple of hours and let you know where we are."

"Make it so." Bully Bear gave Molotov an emphatic nod and then pushed a button under his desk. The heavy steel door clicked twice and then slowly swung open.

Molotov strutted out of the room and convened an emergency meeting with his two most trusted deputies.

Three days later, at dawn, Big Pig's youngest son ran breathlessly into Big Pig's and Voluptua's bedroom, poked Big Pig awake, and asked: "Daddy, why are all the animals pushing against the gates and looking so angry?"

Voluptua, still half asleep, turned over on the white bear rug and muttered drowsily, "What time is it? And why are the curtains drawn?"

Big Pig also noticed the open curtains; he was certain he had closed them only a few hours earlier, before retiring. He clambered out of bed and looked out of the newly installed floor-to-ceiling bay window.

Hundreds of coyotes, cats, prairie dogs, ducks, nine-banded armadillos, chickens, Mexican black bears, gray foxes, Texas longhorns, quails, turkeys, rabbits, goats, horses, pronghorn antelopes, greater roadrunners, white-tailed deer, badgers, beavers, muskrats, ringtails, raccoons, spotted skunks, brown widow spiders–and even a few Western diamondback snakes–had massed outside and were pressing menacingly against the wrought iron gates. In the skies above Animal House, thousands of American crows, Chihuahuan ravens, red-tailed hawks, pigeons, barn swallows, turkey vultures, killdeers, house sparrows, brown-headed cowbirds, red-winged blackbirds, northern mockingbirds, cattle egrets, American coots, cactus wrens, Mexican jays, mourning doves, acorn woodpeckers, and golden eagles were perching themselves on the tree branches and roofs and along all of the power lines and the adjoining properties, while a vast, undulating black cloud of birds appeared on the horizon and, within a few seconds, blotted out the sun.

In the dim, shadowy light, Big Pig could just make out a smaller flock of birds that had broken off from the winged armada and–having swiftly organized themselves into a tight, tip-of-the-spear, "V" formation–were now dive-bombing at prodigious speeds toward the elegant bay window.

The first wave of kamikaze crows smashed against the window with astonishing violence, cracking the plate glass and their own thin skulls and thudding lifelessly onto the blood-spattered patio.

Meanwhile, rhythmic, angry sounds emanated from outside the gates. Big Pig strained to make out what the animals were chanting but was momentarily distracted by a sensation of warm urine trickling down the insides of his hind legs and making little yellow blotches on the white bear rug.

Big Pig herded his terrified wife and son into the hallway. As the threesome clambered toward the Panic Room twenty feet away, neither Big Pig's personal German Shepherd guard dogs nor any of Animal House's regular security detail responded to his shouts for help or were anywhere to be found.

Big Pig pressed his sweaty snout against the state-of-the-art Snout Recognition Screen next to the Panic Room door, but the door did not open. At floor level, he noticed three cut wires running out from a nearby electrical outlet whose thick steel plate had been pried open and, above the plate and taped to the wall, a note with handwriting resembling Silas Cain's.

Penciled on the note were the words, "Every pig has his St. Martin's Day."

Big Pig dropped the note and ran toward the back entrance to Animal House as fast as only a frightened pig can run, oblivious to his wife's shrill cries and his son's terrified, high-pitched squeals.

Voluptua cursed her husband and threw her weight against the Panic Room door, again and again, in a frantic attempt to open it.

The rising chant of the birds and animals outside–augmented by the chorus of maids, cooks, cleaners, managers, construction workers, and security guards who worked at Animal House and who had run out to join them–was now distinctly audible:

"CAGE THE PIG!" "CAGE THE PIG!" "CAGE THE PIG!" "CAGE THE PIG!" "CAGE THE PIG!" "CAGE THE PIG!" …

CHAPTER **10**

In the days and weeks following his unceremoni- ous ouster, Big Pig and his lawyers negotiated a multiparty settlement under which Big Pig would pay money damages to the animal families whose children had been forcibly separated from their parents as part of Big Pig's "zero tolerance" immi- gration policy. Big Pig also made a legally binding commitment that neither he nor any of the com- panies he controlled would file for bankruptcy, anywhere in the world, until all payments to the class of aggrieved animals had been made and that payment in full would include a separate fund to defray the expenses of locating, and reunifying, the two thousand or so members of the dislocated families. In exchange for those payments, the an- imals affected by the forced separations agreed not to file any lawsuit against Big Pig or seek Big Pig's criminal prosecution for assault, battery, child abuse, false imprisonment, or any other crime.

The settlement ensured that Big Pig would serve no jail time but also required him to sell virtually all of his real estate holdings and other assets in order to meet the animals' humongous settlement demands.

And Big Pig had another problem: Bully Bear, who had secretly loaned very large sums to Big Pig and his companies before, and even during, Big Pig's presidency, had called in the loans and demanded immediate repayment. Big Pig knew that his negotiating leverage ended with his presidency and also knew that, unless he repaid Bully Bear in full, and fast, he had best hire a whole team of food tasters, beef up his personal security detail and, if at all possible, get himself inoculated against deadly radioactive nerve agents.

By ten o'clock on the night before the settlement and loan repayments were due, Big Pig had finally secured the needed cash. After all was said and done, Big Pig's sole remaining asset was his Park Avenue apartment in the fashionable Fifties–minus the gold wallow, the gold trough, the gold toilets and bidets, the gold fixtures, the gold clocks, the gold plate, the gold utensils, the gold picture frames, and the gold candelabra, all of which had been auctioned off.

A week after repaying Bully Bear in full, plus penalties and interest, Big Pig received, by first-class international mail postmarked from Moscow, a USB flash drive with an accompanying handwritten note:

"Greetings, Big Pig. A cinematic diversion for you, as you ponder the next phase of your life journey. I hope you enjoy these short videos as much as I and my colleagues have. And if by chance you misplace your flash drive, do not concern yourself. We have others. All the best, Bully Bear"

Big Pig's once-golden brand quickly turned to dross and, in the words of a Stanford professor of business administration reviewing the history of brands in the *Harvard Business Review*, was "a brand that, almost overnight, became as extinct as the dodo bird." With all of Big Pig's buildings and other properties having been sold off at fire-sale prices, none of them now bore his name. In a move that attracted widespread coverage in the *Wall Street Journal* and other human and animal media outlets, Molotov Cocktail's brother, Kolya Molotov, the new owner of the deluxe Manhattan apartment building in which Big Pig resided and which, only a few years before, Big Pig had paid big money to name The Big Pig Power Tower, re-named it, The un-Pig Building.

The post-presidential histories of Big Pig's family were, with two exceptions, unremarkable. Voluptua had confronted Big Pig soon after the election and had struck a devil's bargain with him: during the balance of Big Pig's presidential term, and provided he kept his snout clean and his pecker where it belonged, she would suffer his past serial adulteries and humiliations in silence and otherwise hold her tongue. But once he was no longer president, she would consider herself a free woman and seek the companionship of a better breed of male.

The day after Big Pig's ouster, Voluptua flew to Paris, taking her young son and her longtime personal assistant with her. She promptly filed for divorce on the grounds of adultery and mental cruelty and, after being granted an uncontested divorce decree, married Tenzin Jampa, a virile and distinguished-looking snow leopard who had held high government positions at the Tibetan animal farm and had recently retired to a tasteful duplex apartment near the Champs Elysees. For several years in succession, Voluptua and Tenzin were voted the animal kingdom's most beautiful single-species couple by the readers of *Creature Chic* magazine and could often be seen strolling the tonier boulevards of Paris, their long, elegant tails flirting affectionately as they walked. Voluptua's racy but scrupulously factual memoir, *Pigs in Shit: Living with a Pig President*, became an international bestseller in several animal and human languages and, even many years later, enjoyed brisk annual sales in the United States, Canada, Mexico, the United Kingdom, Ireland, France, Germany, and Australia.

During his father's roller-coaster presidential campaign and short-lived presidency, Big Pig's oldest son had flaunted himself in political and commercial real estate circles as Little Big Pig and had traded lucratively on his famous family connection. But after his father's public disgrace and defrocking, Little Big Pig thought it best to choose discretion over valor, keep his distance, and keep his head down. Little Big Pig let it be known that, henceforth, he would answer only to the name of "Tobias, just Tobias" and moved himself and his young family to a luxury condo somewhere on the Gulf Coast, never to be heard from again.

At Animal Farm and around the world, the animals' decisive actions in ousting Big Pig and throwing off the harsh yoke of pig rule became known as the Second Rebellion. The weeks and months following the Second Rebellion set the stage for a reaffirmation of the basic values of fairness, equality, and common decency that Big Pig had so shamelessly defiled.

A group of elders petitioned Big Pig's predecessors, Sage Raven and Crafty Coyote, to help run the government until a special presidential election could be held. The former presidents agreed to serve in that interim capacity and, wherever possible, to arrive at decisions on a consensus basis. They jointly suggested that a blue ribbon Commission on Reconciliation and Reform be set up (which the two of them would co-chair) to investigate and report on the circumstances surrounding Big Pig's election; to review and remediate the harmful and unlawful actions taken by Big Pig's administration; and to recommend governance reforms that would prevent, or at least inhibit, a recurrence of the Big Pig fiasco.

The Commission's mandate was purposely broad and robust. Sage Raven, Crafty Coyote, and their eleven fellow commissioners (including Henrietta Hen, whose controversial appointment was preceded by a scrappy and often heated internal debate) exploited that breadth in order to try to achieve sweeping reforms which, although sensible and even highly desirable, had previously been considered too politically sensitive to bring forward.

Of the Commission's long list of recommendations calculated to rekindle the constitutional norms and international leadership that Big Pig's chaotic presidency had so spectacularly disrupted–and to reclaim the original conception of Animal Farm as a respectful and peaceable community constituted of the animals, by the animals, and for the animals–the key ones were as follows:

- That all aspirants for the presidency of Animal Farm, prior to declaring their candidacy, be required to demonstrate a working knowledge of the history of the animal rights movement in the United States and internationally; of the laws and constitutional norms of Animal Farm and of how those laws and norms had been interpreted and applied from time to time; of the history of the benign uses and the documented abuses of governmental power over the course of animal and human history; and of the various diplomatic and institutional means by which groups of animal nations, and groups of human nations, had collaborated for the purpose of enhancing not only their collective security against aggressors but also their citizens' economic well-being in an increasingly global marketplace.

- That acceptable proficiency in these core topic areas would be demonstrated by the aspirant's passing, with a score of at least 85%, a written test combining a series of essay and multiple-choice questions devised annually by a nonpartisan, government-funded agency established for that purpose (the "Presidential Competency Test"). If an aspirant declined to take the Presidential Competency Test or failed to achieve the required passing score, he or she would be barred from running for President until a passing score was achieved. (The Commission's private deliberations occasionally threw off some sparks. Sage Raven and Henrietta Hen argued strenuously that the presidential competency bar should be set high and that a presidential aspirant who did not pass the Test on the first try should not be eligible to retake it until the next election cycle. Crafty Coyote strongly disagreed, and exclaimed: "Hey, Sage Raven and Henrietta Hen, not everyone is as smart as you are or has had your high-falutin' educations. Give the rest of us *deplorables* a shot, too, *eh*! Why not give each candidate *three* bites at the testing apple and maybe lower the passing score to, say, fifty-five?" After a spirited and mostly respectful discussion, the Commission unanimously compromised at two test attempts per election cycle but held firm on the 85% passing score.)

- That citizens who are beyond the mandatory school age be given free digital access to the course materials created for the Presidential Competency Test and that a modified curriculum based on those same materials be made part of the mandatory curriculum for all school-age citizens of Animal Farm. (In a footnote to this recommendation, Sage Raven urged that citizens would also profit by becoming familiar with the life, sermons, speeches, and letters of the Reverend Martin Luther King Jr., and with the enduring concept that "Character is fate" first proposed by the Greek philosopher Heraclitus and commented on extensively since then.)

- That all aspirants for the presidency of Animal Farm who pass the Presidential Competency Test be required, no later than two weeks before the election, to make a full public disclosure of their financial holdings and interests, business connections, and family relationships, on a worldwide basis (the "Mandatory Presidential Disclosures"). If an aspirant declined to make the Mandatory Presidential Disclosures or made materially false or incomplete disclosures, he or she would be barred from becoming President. And if false or incomplete disclosures are discovered only after a candidate is elected President, Animal Farm should impose a

mandatory, threefold penalty: (i) immediate removal from office; (ii) a lifetime ban
on holding any future government office at
Animal Farm; and (iii) forfeiture of all of his
or her real property within the jurisdiction
of Animal Farm.

- That, in light of the Commission's findings
documenting the covert steps taken by Bully
Bear and his Sovietski Farm agents, particularly in the social media space, designed to
plant falsehoods and harden existing political
and cultural factions within Animal Farm; to
sow division, disruption, and confusion in the
electorate; and to demonize Henrietta Hen
and enhance Big Pig's prospects for election,
Animal Farm take all necessary security,
technical, and defensive steps to ensure the
fairness and legitimacy of future elections,
including measures and countermeasures to
identify and thwart any malign interference
and to punish the responsible malefactors.

After a series of open-barn meetings held in
communities throughout Animal Farm, followed
by a thirty-day period for written comments, the
Commission's recommendations were put to a
plebiscite vote and, with few exceptions, received
overwhelming support.

The special presidential election held after Big
Pig's ouster was won by an American Mammoth

Jackstock donkey, Grand Canyon, whose hard-scrabble career had featured stints as a wildcat oil driller, a rodeo executive, and an occasional political commentator and who was renowned for his iron resolve, shrewd negotiating skills, and ferocious hind kick.

Grand Canyon's first priority as President was to repair Animal Farm's frayed economic and military alliances with its longstanding animal nation allies in Canada, Mexico, the United Kingdom, Ireland, France, and Germany, and to reaffirm Animal Farm's historic commitment to joint defense of the liberal animal democracies created after the Creature Insurrection.

As his emissaries traveled to Beaverville, Casa Chihuahua, Albion, and the other animal-led communities and began the delicate and painstaking process of diplomatic fence-mending, Grand Canyon took personal charge of administering Animal Farm's immigration policy. Within minutes of his swearing-in, Grand Canyon voided, by Executive Order, Big Pig's "zero tolerance" directive. After consulting with experts on immigration policy and refugee relief, he set up an efficiently run system under which–although Animal Farm would, as a sovereign nation, continue to police its borders–noncitizen animals who had skills needed by Animal Farm, legitimate claims for political asylum, or any other colorable claim to lawful entry into Animal Farm would be treated fairly and with dignity and under no circumstances would any animal seeking entry into Animal Farm be separated from his or her family members. Grand Canyon also ensured that government officials gave all needed assistance to the specially-appointed private individuals who, under the animals' global settlement with Big Pig, were charged with completing the family reunification efforts. (Of the many books written about Big Pig's hateful policy of forced family separations, by far the most compelling was a collection of essays contributed by the family members themselves, titled *Zero Tolerance: Welcome to the Land of the Free and the Home of the Brave!*)

Next, Animal Farm lifted all tariffs on imports imposed by Big Pig's administration—which, after some initial haggling by manufacturers and suppliers on all sides of the international tariff dispute, resulted in the reciprocal lifting of all retaliatory tariffs imposed on Animal Farm's export commodities by Beaverville and other animal nations. And though they issued no "Thank you" to Grand Canyon or his administration, the more virile and sexually active pigs were especially grateful for this outcome—because it made available to them, at market as opposed to black market prices, the specially made, high-end pig condoms that only Beaverville produced (from the recycled hockey pucks) and which Big Pig's trade war had caused Beaverville to stop exporting to Animal Farm.

Grand Canyon's most celebrated accomplishment was his decisive brushback pitch in response to Bully Bear's interference in the election in which Big Pig had squeaked out an electoral college win. Within two weeks of his inauguration, Grand Canyon had assembled an elite team of intelligence, military, and cybersecurity experts and had given them an urgent, twofold task: shore up all of Animal Farm's cyber, telecommunications, and social media networks, defense installations, and power grids, and make them as impenetrable as possible, as quickly as possible; and devise a plan that would make Bully Bear pay a stiff price for his cyber intrusions and deter him from ever trying them again.

Beginning at dawn on the four-month anniversary of Grand Canyon's inauguration, the citizens of Sovietski Farm became crazed with confusion and alarm. Every fifteen minutes for a full twenty-four hours, on every personal computer, tablet, smartphone, television, sports stadium scoreboard, electrically powered sign, and any other surface that could transmit digital images, two short videos appeared in quick succession–and appeared even if the devices' users or controllers made every effort to turn them off: a two-minute video featuring a spot-on likeness of Bully Bear panting in his official throne-chair while he gazed lovingly at the official presidential portrait of Big Pig looking regal and wearing his signature red-white-and-blue presidential sash, with a prominent, flashing caption at the bottom of the screen that read, YOU *STILL* TURN ME ON, BIG PIG!; followed by a one-minute video showing Grand Canyon standing beside the portico of Animal House, looking resolutely into the camera, and declaring confidently:

"Bully Bear, and citizens of Sovietski Farm, this is just a reminder that 'two can play this game.' Please listen carefully. I will say this only once. Don't mess around in Animal Farm's elections or in the elections of our allies. If there is any more of that from you, or from anyone connected with you, my next step will be to hit the "Off" switch on all of Sovietski Farm's electrical, communications, and power grids—and maybe I'll wait until the middle of the Russian winter. And if you doubt that Animal Farm and its allies have the technical means and political will to accomplish that, and much else, just try me. It's your move. I suggest you consider that move *very* carefully."

Bully Bear, after consulting with Molotov Cocktail and other key political and military advisors, thought it best not to try Grand Canyon's patience. Future elections at Animal Farm, although invariably boisterous and hard-fought, proceeded without any malign interference from Bully Bear or any other foreign state actor.

The two presidents who succeeded Grand Canyon placed special emphasis on building stronger bridges to the human community as a means of advancing shared values and trying to slow down global warming and reverse the severe climate gyrations caused by human industrialization. For their part, human environmentalists and scientists stepped up their efforts to develop methods and technologies that would reduce, to more tolerable levels, the amount of carbon dioxide (CO_2) in the atmosphere–recognizing that many of the earth's animal and bird species could not long survive the dramatic changes to their habitats caused by climate change.

During the presidency of Crusty Shell, a nine-banded armadillo who had worked for many years in Arizona and New Mexico as an environmental lawyer before going into politics, a breakthrough occurred. Although the biochemistry and associated technologies were complex and enormously expensive, it was discovered that the natural bodily secretions of four critically endangered species, the Amur Leopard, the Northern Right Whale, the Ivory-Billed Woodpecker, and the Saiga Antelope could, when combined with certain synthetic compounds and sprayed into the atmosphere, cause atmospheric CO_2 molecules to break up and fall back to earth as a mild and unacidic rain.

The leopard, whale, woodpecker, and antelope secretions could not, however, be manufactured or reverse-engineered and much larger quantities were needed to address the atmospheric emergency on an industrial scale. Crusty Shell, along with Bright Beaver, Amelie Eagle, and other animal leaders, knew that real progress on climate change would not only be enormously beneficial to all living creatures but would also reduce the chances of a bloody, worldwide animal insurrection under the battle cry, *Remember the Birds!*

After being briefed by his science advisor and consulting with Animal Farm's closest allies, Crusty Shell negotiated, over many months, a multilateral and multispecies agreement under which–in return for the human governments' binding (and internationally monitored) agreement to drastically reduce greenhouse gas emissions and take more aggressive steps to protect all critically endangered species and their habitats–each animal signatory nation would collaborate with the humans in arranging for the Amur Leopard, Northern Right Whale, Ivory-Billed Woodpecker, and Saiga Antelope populations to breed in safe captivity so that sufficient quantities of their secretions could be generated for the global spraying effort.

Within nine months, large-scale spraying projects were initiated, starting at the two poles, and preliminary CO_2 results were promising. Two years later, the Intergovernmental Panel on Climate Change reported that, for the first time in several decades, average global temperatures were lower than those reported in the prior year and the melt rate of ice in and around the Arctic and Antarctica, and on Greenland's ice cap, had also measurably slowed.

The groundbreaking agreement reached between the Roman Catholic Church and a group of prestigious, animal-led nonprofit organizations called the Consortium for Inter-Species Cooperation and Advancement, or CISCA, was another example of progress between animals and humans in collaborating for their mutual advantage. Pope Nicholas VI had approached Wings, the American eagle who was Chair of the Board of Trustees of CISCA (and who had succeeded Crusty Shell as President of Animal Farm) with an idea that had originated in a feverish dream reported to Pope Nicholas by Cardinal Francis Patrick O'Shaughnessy of Ireland. The Pope, immensely frustrated by the lack of progress he and his predecessors had made in exorcising the shameful legacy of sexual exploitation and abuse by Church officials, hoped to reduce the opportunities for priests, bishops, cardinals, and other Church functionaries to abuse the altar boys and seminarians, and sometimes even the parishioners and fellow priests, with whom they interacted.

As Wings listened respectfully, the Pope explained that the idea was to assign a raven to every priest, bishop, cardinal, or other Church official who was likely to interact, at any time, with any human male or female under the age of twenty-one; and that, conversely, any human male or female under that age who was likely to interact on a regular basis with a Church official—whether as an altar boy, seminarian, office administrator, organist, member of the church choir, student athlete, or what have you—would also be assigned a raven. Could the ravens, the Pope asked, be trained to recognize and react appropriately in situations where either a Church official, or a younger person, exposed any of his or her sexual organs to the other? If so, the Pope went on, future incidents of sexual abuse perpetrated by putative spiritual leaders on children and other vulnerable persons might be curtailed. Would Wings be willing to enlist CISCA's support for this important initiative?

Wings told the Pope that he thought the idea was innovative and had merit but cautioned that a number of logistical details would need to be worked out, including from which animal nations the ravens would be sourced; the optimal training methods for the selected ravens; the length of a given raven's tour of duty; the manner in which the ravens would be compensated; and a host of other details. He agreed to use his influence to garner CISCA's agreement to proceed–provided that the Pope agreed to use *his* influence to reject the inimical Catholic doctrine that, because non-human species are not as "rational" or as "capable of conceptual thinking" as humans, the souls of nonhuman animals are not as spiritually elevated as human souls and are not immortal.

Wings explained to the Pope that, given the sorry mess the humans had made of things, including taking the planet to the very brink of environmental disaster–not to mention the Roman Catholic Church's own contemptible record of enabling rampant child sexual abuse by Church officials–the worldwide animal community could no longer accept being regarded as immutably inferior beings unworthy of the Creator's equal concern and respect. (Wings was also tempted to tell the Pope that, if he really doubted whether animals have capacious souls, he should get himself a pet dog or a pet cat or take up riding horses.)

Although it took several months for the mutual accommodations to get worked out, the Catholic Church ultimately relented, the assigned ravens were vigilant and effective, and the so-called Guardianship by Ravens program was considered a resounding success. Indeed, CISCA was also approached by a group of human leaders from the #MeToo movement in the United States, Canada, and Europe–who asked whether it would be possible for ravens to discharge similar duties in connection with male supervisors, on the one hand, and female workers of all ages, on the other, in human stores, office buildings, executive suites, government buildings, courts of law, police stations, sports facilities, television and movie studios, Boy Scout and Girl Scout troops, hotels, schools, universities, print and electronic media outlets, military installations, and on the shop floors of industrial plants.

In only one recorded instance was a raven constrained to peck and gouge the exposed, engorged penis of a man of the cloth. After a full investigation by lawyers retained by the Vatican, the raven in question was cleared of any wrongdoing; was found to have uttered, at least three times, the standard "*raack-raack-raack*" warning to the pedophile priest, before striking; and was commended for his spirited defense of the eleven-year-old altar boy.

The obituaries recording Big Pig's passing were numerous and unapologetically blunt. The number of animals and humans who attended his funeral was, however, few. Try as they might, Big Pig's descendants could convince no one but themselves that his funeral had been attended by the largest number of animals and humans ever to attend the funeral of a former President of Animal Farm.

Upon learning of this bogus claim, the editors of *The Animal Times*–the animal kingdom's largest-circulation daily newspaper translated in all of the principal animal languages–wrote:

"One of the many enduring lessons our citizens learned from Big Pig's toxic presidency is the importance of grounding government policy on facts and evidence rather than on slogans and demagoguery, including the simple but valuable lesson that a large number is, and always will be, larger than a smaller one. Big Pig's daily, shape-shifting deluge of lies, malice, confusion, propaganda, misogyny, racism, and xenophobia caused us to forget or undervalue many important things which, happily, we have since learned to remember and to cherish. But even during those dark and tumultuous days, we never forgot 'how to count.' And if asked to opine on an appropriate epitaph for Big Pig's tombstone, we would suggest the following: 'Here lies Big Pig, a disgraced and disgraceful President, who tirelessly gave the citizens of Animal Farm ever-new and enraging reasons to hate their government.'"

Virtually all of the obituaries and commentaries about Big Pig and his failed presidency proceeded in the same caustic vein. The animal edition of *Time* magazine declared that "Big Pig was confident in proportion to his vast ignorance"; that his "wild blunders were the product of a sophomoric and dangerously disordered mind"; and that "he seemed to hate the citizens of Animal Farm for the very wrongs he had done to them."

Only a few revisionist, right-wing media outlets pushed the contrarian view that Big Pig had been woefully misunderstood and ill-treated during his time in office; that, had Big Pig only been given more time, his "shrewd domestic and geopolitical chess moves" would have enhanced animal freedom and prosperity in the United States and abroad; and that Big Pig's greatness would, in the fullness of time, be validated by history.

Years passed.

Big Pig had long since died in exile and had lived out his remaining years in his Park Avenue apartment–ranting, on *and* off the golf course and to anyone who would listen, that his unceremonious ouster had been hatched by a "Deep State" conspiracy orchestrated by the fiendish Henrietta Hen and her scheming retainers, and abetted by the sinister machinations of Sage Raven and *his* scheming retainers.

Bully Bear had also long since died, not in exile or of natural causes, but from lethal complications resulting from accidental exposure to a weapons-grade radioactive nerve agent. Molotov Cocktail–who had succeeded Bully Bear as President of Sovietski Farm and, soon thereafter, invested himself with the titles, Supreme Leader and Creature Hero, First Class–had promised the citizens of Sovietski Farm a full and fair investigation, but the circumstances surrounding Bully Bear's mysterious death were never disclosed.

Since the Second Rebellion, the presidency of Animal Farm had been discharged by a wide variety of species, including a donkey, an armadillo, an American eagle, a Calico cat, a Clydesdale horse, an American spider beetle, and two Golden Retrievers. The canine species had enjoyed a particularly strong run in recent years: the incumbent President of Animal Farm, a Havanese, had recently been re-elected to a second presidential term in the largest electoral landslide in the nation's history.

During that long span, no pig had achieved the presidency of Animal Farm or of any other animal nation. Indeed, no pig had even declared his or her candidacy for the presidency, and not for lack of political ambition. On the question of their perceived fitness for high government office, the pigs at Animal Farm, Beaverville, Albion, and other animal-led communities were forced to accept that they had not yet paid the price for the sins of their proverbial forefathers and that it was a very open question whether the non-pig majorities would ever consider that price to have been paid in full.

And much to the chagrin of the pigs and their well-heeled retainers, the earlier prophecy that Big Pig's greatness would one day be validated by history found no support in the retrospective assessments of historians. To the contrary, Big Pig's despotic misrule–and the comparable despotism of the pigs who had seized control of the original animal farm in England more than a century before–were now the subjects of lengthy chapters in all of the assigned elementary, high school, and university history books and even the less-formally-educated animals had come to appreciate the practical importance of that unsentimental education.

The citizens of Animal Farm USA were not always sure what they wanted, or didn't want, from their government. But on one point they were overwhelmingly agreed: *under no circumstances did they want the pigs back.*

To be sure, pigs continued to play leading roles in Animal Farm's business sector; aggressively solicited and exploited business opportunities both within and beyond Animal Farm; and were, as before, disproportionately represented on lists of the world's richest animals. But Big Pig's program of shameless self-dealing, gratuitous malice, and abuse of power had helped the animals (including some of the younger pigs approaching voting age) to understand that prudent governance of a nation requires its leaders to embrace an ethical stance and worldview more encompassing than the morals of the marketplace. Grand Canyon, in his commencement speech to the first graduating class from Animal Farm's Cyber & Polytechnic Institute, ably summarized the still-generally-held view: "We must never again submit to being ruled by pigs. Let the past be no prologue!"

As the trauma inflicted by Big Pig's presidency faded from year to year; as the politics of Animal Farm USA gradually returned to at least a measure of normalcy, where competing presidential candidates and their supporters once again regarded themselves more as political opponents with differing policy views than as implacable enemies; and as the Commission's key reforms produced, over time, a richer and more qualified pool of presidential candidates and a more educated and enlightened electorate, the citizens of Animal Farm tended to elect presidents who, regardless of their party affiliation, competed for high government office in order to get some constructive things done for the nation and its citizens, rather than to stoke their vanity, massage their egos, elevate their personal brands, enrich themselves and their friends, or set the table for lucrative careers on cable TV.

Late in her historic tenure as the first female President of Animal Farm USA, Matilda—a wise and empathetic Havanese dog whom everyone called Tilly—marshaled support for convening a special session of the International Congress of Free Animals. The purpose of the session was to devise a Universal Declaration of Animal Rights to which each animal nation would subscribe, followed by enactment of local laws ensuring enforcement of the Declaration in each animal-led community.

With Tilly assuming the role of Drafter-in-Chief, and following prolonged and vigorous discussions involving a large number of drafts and amended drafts, the Congress approved the following Universal Declaration of Animal Rights:

ALL ANIMALS ARE EQUAL AND NONE IS MORE EQUAL THAN OTHERS

At the ensuing press conference, Deep Furrow, a Pulitzer-Prize-winning German Shepherd reporter from *The Animal Times,* asked the first question:

"Madam President, given that the humans have such greater propensity, and such greater capacity, for destroying the planet, do you think they might someday adopt and enforce a similar Declaration and, in so doing, prevent an unhappy end for all of us?"

Tilly paused, thanked Deep Furrow for his probing question, and ambled up to the microphone:

"In my experience, the humans are like little children. They can all learn, some more quickly than others. They need to be taken gently by the hand, guided in the ways of the world, and taught what is good for them and what is not good for them. And though some of them are selfish, stupid, and even cruel, most of them have no wish to harm others or to harm the planet and become responsible citizens. Unfortunately, and like some of the animals from our own checkered history, humans who show early signs of outsized selfishness and cruelty often grow up with a strong will to dominate others. Later in life, some of them seek high political office as a means of exercising that domination. When that happens, things never end well. Happily, the humans have got better at choosing leaders who, whatever their other faults, are not dangerously selfish, stupid, or cruel. And it is also true that the animal communities represented at this Congress have, over time, become not only wiser, but kinder. To quote the Reverend Martin Luther King Jr., the arc of the moral universe seems, of late, to be bending a little more toward justice–and, I would add, toward the preservation of our planet. So there is reason for hope."

Lightning Source UK Ltd.
Milton Keynes UK
UKHW011302170520
363416UK00003B/8/J